THE LEGEND OF NEKRóS LIEWEG

SUKHVIR SONI

This book is dedicated to me and my imagination.

~Imagine it your way~

Yeah, There is a challenge here, you have to find these words with wrong spelling which can be anywhere in this book!

1)challange
2)fingure
3)frustated
4)fullfil
5)intreasted
6)medatative
7)possibily
8)reffering
9)showes
10)shued

Contents

Introduction

Introducing you to Ajax a young and dedicated man who starts his journey to the island of Nekrós Leiweg. A legend describes about, "An island holding Magical abilities". Ajax with a strong desire to find the truth and meet the dreams of his grandfather has to clear beaucoup number of Dangers. A Poem in the form of a riddle and prophecy, to guide him to his journey. The Legendary book "Lareme" to helps and the creature no where to be seen. The mysteries arise as the strongest Ruler revives, the danger increase, but he has help. A Royal history it has, but, it had end, only to rise again. The things to find to help them all, but it keeps on getting hard as the time pass.

Acknowledgements

I got inspired by my friends, other fictional book, series and movies. I too maked a lot of mistakes in the book but at last all of then were covered. I hope you enjoy and yeah, you can always skip to the chapter...

Preface

So if you are reading this you are not yet introduced to the main character, or maybe you are. Anyways he is strong, capable and pure of Heart. You are going to love the adventure of this island and more. He and others worked hard to get were they are, and to acheive what they did, so I would like to suggest you all the same, "Never Give Up."

Prologue

Wind is blowing, leaves are moving, I can smell the grass, hear the ocean, and feel the possibilities.

He opened his eyes and was already ready to go!

Foreword

The Poem it will help!

You can write hear anything, ofcourse if you want to!

CHAPTER ONE

Challenges for Magical Desire

In the middle of the ocean, A young man named Ajax sailed to the water of North Atlantic ocean. ("Ajax was in a boat which was between 12 and 15foot with all the necessary thing, Many things in general and a Brown bag in specific.") The time is close! he said and waited for a second looking at the sky. Ajax waited, until he closed his eyes and sang in his mind...

"Here he come!"
With courage and determination
To a Island unknow only to form a mission
"Nekrós Lieweg" goes on it's name
An island full of creatures impossible to tame
The Island which once was great
Vanishing dead excepting it's fate
The one known to some for Mysteries, Power and Magic.
But who dares to enter, dies a death full of tragic.
'Yes' it is still as alive,
But 'no one here' to form an hive.
The Adventure Starts here :-

'Lightning striked' and that was the exact moment He opened his eyes, He took a rope 'in hurry' and tied it's one end to the front of the boat while other in his hands. When he was singing, It started to rain, "The waves grew bigger and bigger". It didn't took him a second to figure out, Storm is here and his struggle to survive has started. It was raining hard and there would almost be no hope to survive, the huge waves were coming ahead but Ajax was still determined, knowing who he was. He first covered all his stuff with a blue carpet, While riding the boat like it was a horse. "At that same moment he saw another boat with 3 to 5 people in it, they were wearing an armour which looked strong". As the waves grew bigger it became more difficult for him and soon he could see it the Biggest wave coming towards him. He said "I havn't seen a wave as big as this one", It wasn't long before the wave approached him and a matter of fact he was seeing it as a Golden opportunity... He took his stance holding the rope firmly just a feet away from the beginning of the boat, where it was tied. There It was a big wave followed by a Humongous one, He was already on a height, riding the big wave. Ajax waited for the perfect moment and when he was an inch away to touch the upper part of the humongous wave. He jumped at the end of the boat while releasing the rope until he was at the end, Right when he was in the middle of jumping, he threw a mini depth charge(Water bomb) made by him and his brother, with full power and speed, Which just after a second Blast strong. The Blast made him gain height which enabled him to use his boat like a surfing board in a unique way. As his boat was higher from front, 'due to his weight when he jumped at end holding the rope', He landed on the Humongous wave very smoothly, but his boat got a little damaged from bottom. "Yeaahh" he screamed while cleverly controlling his boat, he surfed the water like a Champian. It didn't took long for the Thunderstorm to end and a bright fresh Day was waiting ahead. All this thing looked like a matter of minutes, Yeah to him too, But 37minutes was the time it took, fighting the thunderstorm and the waves. He was checking that all his stuff was in one piece. Then having patience he was sitting with legs cross and taking long breath, trying to relax his body, when he saw. "A moment in the water" It was like ("he felt") many things were going to approache him. His instinct was right! It was barely 5minutes escaping the deadly Thunderstrom and here a new trouble arrives. Ajax looked around in the water until he stopped at a point. He was seeing the water as something slowly was coming towards him. The thing jumped out of water scaring Ajax. It was something like a shark but not one exactly, "It was different". Let me tell you, it is a Unique creature which looks exactly as a shark but is Dark Black in color. The species name is türemgii, They are know for their Aggression in The Book of Lamere... Ajax was terrified and removed The Legendary Book of lamere, at least that's what he thought. "Lamere 'The Guide' was written of the front cover of the book in Golden letters, the book was written by an unknown Author" He turned pages and found the knowledge about türemgii, ("The type of shark not known to be found, no ordinary person is known to have lived the attack of türemgii. The dark Protector, who wont think twice before killing anybody disturbing the laws. The hot minded creature known for their aggression is a true danger for all creatures alike. Beware of the teeth, "immortal till life", they can easily break most of the metals. The speedy creature can swim faster than many other marine life. All it's feature would make it impossible to defeat, But there still are things to get it through. You may know that the türemgii are very sensitive with their tail, they are scared to lose or even hurt their small tail. The less brains are also scared from people who can fly or the people who can some how levitate or at least show them they are. The türemgii think them as God, They can be loyal to them and by showing them You are stronger than them, the chance will be a 92% more. You should keep in mind that türemgii have weak eyes and by attacking it, they can be distracted. Known impossible to tame, but if, It would let free, and start building the thing inside. ~One may die for the other life~") was written in the book. Ajax, anyways just read the needed information again and there he was ready to face the danger ahead. He took his Sword "SBA-GLADIUS-VESPARUM" and waited for them to attack so he can strike off their tail. He soon saw a group of 4 coming towards him, He was ready but was continuously thinking. One of them jumped at him and he moved his strong hands, "He missed" the book was write The türemgii changed its path by a little, just to save its tail. Ajax was furious, but he damaged it a little, resulting it to slow down. He was striking them down one by one as more were coming to attack him. His boat was getting damaged by the constant attack of türemgii, He was worried because of what he saw. He saw a hundred of them from a farther distance coming right for him. A second of distraction, was all it needed to accidentally drop a depth charge from his bag which got opened by the side a little from the constant biting of the water creatures. Ajax tried his best to move his boat away from the place where the incident was going to take place, and somewhat succeeded. "Boooom" the depth charge exploded injuring many of them, and frightening others a little. It didn't effect Ajax though, he was still thinking, still thinking about an idea. It would be hard he said, And just after that he removed a medium pack of salt from one of his bag and kept it aside. He then quickly removed the gift given by his fellow professor, Who happens to be his elder sibling, name of this brilliant brain "Albert". Ajax opened it up in curiosity as he already knows what's inside it... The gift happens to be a plate, 'no ordinary one' a magnetic plate made of strong neodymium magnet, There was another bag attached to the plate one. The other bag had 2shoes both made of neodymium magnet with very strong magnetic force of repulsion. Ajax wore the shoes without wasting any further time and the explosion gave him some extra of it. He then took a wooden box with metals inside he bought along and placed the magnetic plate on it. Time was running and all the türemgiis were coming, coming to kill him, at least for now. He, Furthermore, Removed a glove which He and his brother worked on some days prior, and wore it in his left hand. Ajax took a long breath and jumped on the plate which caused him levitate with the help of science and not magic, this time. The time could not be better as the türemgiis were coming at full speed and stopped seeing him in air. He bend down and picked up the pack of salt, He was often about to fall but controlled. He opened the bag of salt and started throwing it in their eyes. All the türemgiis were curiously frightened, They all backed off and swam away from Ajax, they swam as fast as they were swimming for their life. It was an opportunity for him to escape and he paddled his paddle and moved away. "It has been more than 10minutes now but Ajax has just moved a little near 100m as he is now resting for like 6minutes now. Although he has placed all his stuff, each and everyone of them inside a big strong bag made of double layered leather, in the mean time. He was drinking water from his old looking copper bottle when he started to feel strong winds, much stronger than before. Ajax now finally started to move ahead. Now now, you would be thinking how can someone just keep moving ahead without knowing where he was going? and "What is going on?" To know the answer read this and imagine something singing it for you...

"700years ago",
it has been revive
It's all a game of Dead-Alive
The number which shall show it's importance
With Him, who impresses with it's performance
"She" who 'Sees It All'
Is believed, Long Ago has fall
First, "The Impossible waves to be surfed"
can only be defeated by a real Versed
The Large number with Teeths and Beaks
Double Trouble, For him who seeks
The Painful truth flowing in the mind
Destroying stability all it can find
Reaching there the view you see
It may repeat, yet with a cup of tea.

This poem is some-kind-of magic a type of magic done on The Book of Lamere to make it sing. It's hard to understand, only a few ordinary has yet and by few it means way less than a dozen, Ajax listened to it many time before coming for this Unique adventure, infact he was singing the poems almost all the time in his mind. Ajax was starting to catch his pace when he saw a huge unrecognizable and unorganized figure rising up from the far-away water. It was all up like a widely spread peace of land flying up in the sky from a distance very far from him. Ajax was starring at the sky when he started to understand the Poem/Riddle/Guide or whatever it is. Most people would be fearful or worried by the situation but our Hero was anxious to unravel the mystery up ahead. He took out his sword "SBA-GLADIUS-VESPARUM" and held it firmly in his right hand. He thought he should remove his other sword which was way better than any other in existence with many enchanted supernatural power, But again he saved it for later. Ajax was sure when he saw the figure rising up that it was a massive piece of land, He just didn't have a proper explanation for it. And now as the Black Patch in the sky comes closer, He was sure it was S-o-m-e-t-h-i-n-g else. He speedily removed his binoculars and was stunned of what he saw, So it is it he said. Just after that he removed the book 'Yeah you guessed it', The book named Lamere. Turned some pages again and here:-("Turba Inimicus" The Dark Blue coloured creature, with height between 1.9 to 2.3 feet. The less Brain creatures are known to live in big group, A group mostly consists of a 100 or more of their species. Turbas would make a big crowd only when instructed or for an emergency situation. They can fly through a speed of 65miles per hour with their pointy wings, and their Red Bloody eyes are enough to remove the hell out of a weak person. Turba Inimicus have long red coloured beak with shades of black in it. Mainly they have a pair of 3 claws which can easily boost the fear of anybody trying to face one. 'With any great features comes a weakness' and these weakness would be enough to kill them. First remember there sharp claws and strong Beaks, They wont attack someone with fire near them. One of the biggest weakness for them is High Pitched sound which has to be loud often to loud to cause any damage, It can usually confuse them and would encourage them to fly away. But, They aren't the weakest one so, There are chances some will resist the suffering, and the only option left would be to cut their head off "Kill them". ~Attacking attack for once allegiance~.) Ajax, However was ready, With matches and lighter and the inborn ability to make irritatingly loud sound. All The Turba Inimicus were getting close and it was like a 1 vs 1100 match, Yeah there were 1100 of them that's what Ajax estimated and his estimation was almost right. Ajax lit his torch and held it in his left hand and the sword in other, He stood up as he was a Chosen one and give a strong smile before starting the fair war. With a burning torch and a powerful sword he felt like he was invincible but there's the twist. "The Dumb Angry Birds were not just by themselves, They were carrying Arrows." Ajax realized when he saw them from a closer distance. He was feeling defeated but determined and curious at the same time, He still haven't given up the hope and his mind was still in his control. The day was no longer bright or sunny. He saw up as the crowd was just a second away to through the sharp pointy arrows, He closed his eyes and jumped in the water, turning his boat upside down. He opened his eyes from under the water and saw everyone throwing thousands of arrow on him. He swam under his turned boat and took a long breath and went straight below the turned boat, taking the blue carpet with him. Ajax wrapped the carpet around him covering almost all of his body as he was seeing the view of his boat getting destroyed but the doubled layered leather bag saved all the stuffed inside it. It was a truly heartwarming moment as "Ajax down underwater was constantly getting hit by arrows thrown by 1000+ Turbas on the surface of water and the thing that made it all more extraordinary was a Big flying figure which was wandering on top of the turned boat shooting Hot Fire all around the surface of water and above. The matter of fact, The Figure happens to be none other than The "Dragon", Ajax was seeing all the thing. A painful yet pleasing thing to feel according to him..." He almost ran out of breathe, but just before the attack was stopped, He came up and took a long breathe from the warm water with nothing much to float on, as the boat was destroyed. He climbed on the pieces that were left out. Shortly after that he took a dive in the ocean and bought the bag full of his stuff up on the surface. For a moment he was relieved seeing nothing more than the sun setting down in the sky but these thing destroyed his hope, or. He looked up seeing all the Turbas coming for him and was he tired enough to fight back, fight back without any major weapon against them. But at the same moment he saw the Legendary Dragon coming for him too, He got an idea to use the dragons flames against the crowd to take down the lot. The Dragon came closer very fast as well as Turbas but some seconds was all it needed to take a small wet piece of wood floating nearby. He stood up on two wooden piece, kept one on another with the small wood piece in his hand and when the Dragon was close enough to use it's inbuilt flamethrower Ajax threw the wooden piece in the air and jumped in the water. Dragons have strong vision-power, he saw it and launched his flamethrower on the wooden piece causing the Turbas to back off. He then again stood up, The sun nearly set, And he was seeing the Dragon in his eyes as it was Flying. The Dragon 'saw the man', looking back in the eyes and for a second it was like Both of them were connected by some force a Strong Aura. Ajax remembered the tales that his Grandfather used to say to him. Suddenly, The Turba's attacked the Dragon and continued to make him weak but our Dragon was not a Baby! He replied back like a fierce warrior. And in a couple of minutes killed all of them showing no mercy, Our Hero Ajax knocked a hundred or little less too with the help of his depth charges. It was Dark and the dragon left, leaving Ajax alone with a total weight of almost a 100kg, with the pieces of the broken boat. He was yet not to give up and continue to struggle a bit long only to fulfill a strong desire. He was all alone for more than 20minutes now, Hungry, Tired, Lonely and Cold. He waited for some rocks to show up so that he could rest and remove his electrical torch so see things. It took him another 24minutes to find one but at least he did, finally. Ajax sat on one of them and removed a torch and a translucent empty container, He switched on the torch and placed it inside the container, Making a DIY lamp. "I can finally see things now" he said not in excitement and removed some packed food to eat. He was happily eating the food when he saw some small yellow crystals on the big enough rocks, which happens to be Sulphur. He started to wonder, If Sulphur is here that could mean I am near a piece of land, Perhaps an Island. Could it be he said to himself and gave a big laugh. Which unfortunately happens to be the only one in recent, he heard a loud roar, louder than Lion. He was irritated and frustrated till now with no ability to see by tiredness but the consequences made him satisfied and gave birth to a new hope. "Roarrrrrr" The sound came again and even louder this time, it was as if the beast was closer now. He started to put all his stuff back and turn off the torch, But he has to hurry. He wrapped all his stuff but the last roarrr he heard was loud as it was less than 30feet away. Ajax was hearing gruffs of more than one of whatever beast it was, He took his stance with his sword in one hand. He heard the loudest roar yet and flashed on the Beasts orange eyes forming a scary image in his brain. The beast was attacking Ajax without a sweat which caused him to drop his torch write in front of a mirror he didn't knew existed. This small incident caused a very bright light, Ajax for the first time saw the face of the beast and quickly recognized who it was. It was Sthenarós Milos a Real Beast, almost 10feet tall, Colour changing Orange eyes, Two Big Teeth sharp and light Grey in color like a sabertooth tigers but much bigger and stronger. They were like Lions but twice as big as them, They have a tail which was split in half from the beginning and joining again with a furry end. It was written in The Book Of Lamere that:- Sthenarós Milos a Truly wonder Beast "It used to be", Milos are very protective for the one who they care and Their decrease in population had increased this ability even more. Sthenarós Milos is a very Strang and Powerful creature, His two Legs and Arm filled with muscle power and They use it in strenuous ways against their enemies. They can run at incredible speed of 80 to 120miles an hour, These creature are intelligent not as much as a human but they can be classified in highly understanding creatures. It is known that only a few 20 to 30 of them are alive in the whole world. They don't trust anyone and are Proud of themselves. The most interesting thing, It is believed that they can manipulate and even control the one who looks in their eyes for long, if they want. These creatures don't have many weakness, but there sure are some. Note:- Their skin is very strong and hence, very difficult to damage or peel of. Milos head, That's the place to strike your sword or other strong and sharp weapon. This is hard but you can test your inner energy, if Sthenarós tries to control you, you can check it by starring in its eyes hard. A suggestion! Don't kill any of these creature as they are endangered and 'not Evil', but if important try the things instructed before and by-chance if not successful then try all you can to damage it till it dies, Which can take some serious Time. Ajax was confused as Both the Sthenarós were straining their eyes due to the increasing light. The light was increasing and Ajax could feel warm on his body, The Sthenarós suddenly ran away as the light was seriously increasing now. Ajax was afraid he would go Blind if it dosen't stop, he covered his eyes but the Heat was still increasing. "Booom" The torch exploded and Ajax felt that "He was falling, Falling deep". After some second he started to see visions. He saw, His Grandfather cutting wood and there was people around them minding there own business when he was 6. Ajax was walking when he fell deep into a hole with some snakes in it, crawling all over his body but not hurting him. He was rescued after 25 to 30minutes and when was removed out already fainted he was. The thing his grandfather was telling him was mystifying, Queer and rather bit of Magical, It hurted him and remained in his mind as his grandfather never talked about it again. Ajax after that saw his memory when he was 8, getting bullied by Teenager. Getting hit seve ral times and after they were gone, him falling in a river. Drowning as the memories of him, flashes before his inward eye, The last thing he remember was a face, He described scary. He woke up at night after being rescued by a creepy unknown glowing figure. His memory then switched to another one, This time More Alone, Dark and Painful. This memory is kept concealed in his mind by himself because this memory was unbearable for Ajax. The memory flowed like this, "He was standing in a room Dark, Alone, Scared and Empty." He just started to forcefully see this worst memory, when he felt Angry, Fearful and Aggresive. It was not the first time when he felt so vulnerable. Just seeing him standing in a hair-raising room with a horrific feeling is to much for a 12year old. In real time Ajax don't want to remember it, Ajax painfully and Angrily screamed 'Nooooooo'. He really would have control over his mind cause the memory switched to another one without talking the last memory any further. Ajax was hoping to be in this memory. He always thought of this, just after the incident took place. But this memory always makes him "lost, Sad and a little engrossed". He saw his grandfather great and unusual, Giving him a gift, "A gift he said to open only at a time it is required like nothing before, A Time you think is the perfect for a perticular thing, you may know when the time comes or 'you do'." It was the few last moment of Ajax and his family with his Grandfather. It is almost time Ajaxs father said, Yeah-Yeah "None fascination more than me", Ajaxs grandfather replied. He gave gifts to all the family members, his grandfather. And he was just about to sail far away than here when he shared a few past memories with both of his grandsons. He said to both of them, "I am sure you both will take care of yourselves, That's obvious. And it will be good if you both wont tell about our short crazy adventure we just had an hour ago. Both laughed and Albert added it was dangerous too you know with a smile. Suddenly Ajax stopped laughing and said You will come back, Right? Sure I will! old man replied. But you may not go, "It doesn't represents us", Plus you are already 84 andd... I know I know no need to say their grandfather replied. He came closer to their ears and said "It's not Important to be the Chosen on", You just need to beleive in yourself. After saying he hoped on the boat moving ahead while looking at them. He said, his last words, Don't worry for me 'Everyone dies' one day, "Even the immortals". And you know "I am no-way near weak". And always remember this "A fleeting death for a persistent living!" He was a distance further than everybody when a lightning stroke on his boat and he was no-where to be seen, Everyone believed him to be Dead, and all this happened when Ajax was 16. Ajax was Heartbroken, Standing without a moment and Felt Ruthless to the path of what he desire for his Grandfather. The reason of showing him these memory was of-track, It was meant to destroy his hope but Instead. It went a little different and Utterly unexpected. It seems, Ajax was gaining some sort of energy from all these things he felt and was storing it incognizantly. The last memory he saw, procured him enough power to Blast it off in Real Time. Ajax, when was going through the emotional suffering was actually sinking in a sand, He was in Time as he just sinked till his neck. It was a sand different than other, A type of quicksand which will sink anybody who sets a foot in it. It is made by one who knows Magic, By some difficult and roomy brewing. After the Sand is made it has to be placed on a perticular place, till it is removed from there. The sand works like this. It traps the victim just if He/She steps into it. The sand will start paralysing ones body and eventually turn into Hard Stone, Immposible to break, "Slowly". It will show the most painful memories they have, only 5 to 15minutes have past for the victim but it would be hours. Mostly the one inside will sleep at the beginning but I believe it is even wore. "This is what written in Lareme". Ajax Although Broke the unbreakable mainly because of his stored power and him being extraordinary. He was free and Opened his eyes, he saw it was almost morning as he was getting a cool view of the Sunrise. He was facing the ocean remembring that he has survived all the attacks, "He was so happy", when he remembered to turn back. He looked behind and saw the View he would never forget in a 100Billion years.

CHAPTER TWO

Stories and the Time to Think

He First saw a Volcanic Mountain, Very big with it's position more at Left. Followed by cool clouds and the creature Flying through them. He could also see the Ruins of the Village, abandoned long ago. He also was able to see the 'Great Tower' brocken now. He could see the immense Island with different sections erratically divided. The flowers, fruits and the Creatures Extraordinary and not to be found anywhere else, fascinated him. It was like a fantasy but for Ajax it was a part of his dream that came true. He was still on the outskirt of the Island on a big piece of rock filled with The sand from before and only some meters away to enter "The Island called Nekrós Lieweg." He knew a new early era is here which will be dangerous, it is like first set of trouble and riddle is complete. With him survived and the next is going to be something more big. He first got out of the small hole conjure by himself. Then reached the close-by rock to take his big bag, full of his Stuff. He with the bag quite heavy started to move forward into the island. He walked ponderously towards the island but wasn't sad, He instead was determined and walking in his placidness without anything disturbing his tranquillity for a serene amount of time. It was a moment never to be stopped peaceful to look and to experience. In 10 to 15minutes he was there on the Island where Ocean water can't reach. He saw the ocean and walked for the tree he could see from the distance up. Some moment later he was there a place looking safe and on some height. It was the place where he wanted to eat the food he brought along or the fruit on the tree. He went for his food and started eating, he was done after some minutes when he thought. He should try the fruit as it looked similar to apple with some differences, and he did so only one fruit from a unknown tree. It tasted sweet, when he heard footsteps of big animal coming towards him. He closed his eyes and tried to sense from where it was coming, He got it and prepared himself, removing his sword from it's scabbard and was ready to react to any attack. They were approaching him from the back and were just about to hit Ajax with their horns when he jumped aside. It was nosorog, also known as rhinoceros. But there is a difference here, these rhinoceros were slightly big with stronger bodies. there face was little bit like a normal hippopotamus with two dotted nose and a big mouth. They too have one horn of white or grey color, and are inborn experts in using them. These nosorog's are usually calm and territorial creatures and they live with their crash near a source of water and trees. The nosorog's were inquisitive and vexed, They thought Ajax was stealing their on-tree food and encroach in their territory. Both Ajax and all the Nosorog were standing still seeing in each others eyes, both waiting for another one to attack. Ajax started to bow down showing his respect, Which would have forced them to think twice, he was picking the stone below at the same time. He then started to stand straight with head up and threw his sword away. Seeing this the Nosorogs were confused and started to think "he is not dangerous". Ajax, knew about them quite well, all thanks to The Book of Lamere. He, However was in a mood for some fun. Ajax then removed a berry from his pocket and threw it in front of them. The poor creature had no idea what he was doing so one of them came ahead to smell it, When she was smelling the berry. Ajax jumped on the tree and climbed on one of the strong branch. The Nosorog was furious but had a merciful feeling inside. Ajax had knowledge about nature, trees, Fruits, Animals ect too. So he pulled some fruits and throwed them towards the little ones. The Nosorog were really confused now, Their anger decreased, because he was up on the tree. Ajax then removed a water ballon from his pocket, which nosorogs thought was interesting, he filled the balloon with water when he still was on rocks and kept it in his pocket with the stone he just picked. He then throwed the balloon up and aimed it with the stone. The balloon popped and the water was spilled in the air, as the nosorogs were seeing it. Just by seeing the balloon pop made all of them happy, it is a simple phenomenon. Listen! When something that reflects light like water is thrown upwards, for an example, Light gets reflected through its surface producing a flash. These sparkle release a hormone called Dopamine, Which eventually makes people happy. And, When this happens with Nosorogs they become happy more than any human in the world, by this particular method. The water droplets fell on them and till the time they could realize what was going on Ajax was gone, at least for them. In real he was behind the tree, removing a basket full of apples from his bag. They all were looking for him desperately,

Which was when he shooked everybody by hopping from behind the tree. He then slowly moved ahead towards the crash and placed the basket in front of them. Soon after an infant came ahead and took a bite. By seeing him others joined and started to finish it all. Ajax was soo content and happy seeing this. He came ahead and tamed one of the Nosorogs followed by others and they showed their affection by licking him all over. He backed off and went towards his big bag with his stuff, telling them "Gotta go now, we will meet again". When he sliped on his right to show nosorogs some trick and jumped down the slope. Only to know that he has to pay big time for his acting. He was sliding down without control, when a stone came in the way and he rolled down intractable falling in a hole. The hole happens to be a slide to a cave not fully formed naturally, not at all. He slided deep in and found himself deep down, He was deep underground. Ajax landed in the cave, dark underground cave and he not having any source of light, 'not even his extra emergency one', became clueless. He started to move around to see how much space was available inside, as he could not see a thing. He moved his hands to feel an objects presence or the wall ahead. It was a big area. Ajax suddenly was daze and sat down in a shook, He realized it could be the end. Then, he thought about the second one, the poem in the guide, the one with clues and the knowledge to decrease the element of surprise of the nature of this island.

The Great Ruler for the rise
and the sacrifies ahead that lies
The need of blood to fulfill the thirst
for the curse to be marked the first
The knowledge that you-may-know
with the hidden treasure, below
Together for all till the end
may the help for you be lend
The things you will know from deep inside
to fight the Power for everyones pride
Everything you see left from the past
Clues to be found, for the one last

He remembered the poem and somewhat knew what to do. First of all he needed light to see what exactly was the situation around him and 'to find it'. The "Ancient Text", it is a masterpiece left by the people of the Queen and The Queen herself. Ajax had an idea of what will be on the stone walls of the deep cave, as by the stories he had heard from his Grandfather and the knowledge he gained from the book. He started to move around and came across a wall with some different stones in it, these stones are smooth he said. He then used his muscle power and detached two of them from the unorganized structure of this cave. He had a false hope that it was Flint. 'Crash', He rubbed the stone together, nothing happened. He rubbed again and again and there it was, A spark of hope. It was conformed to him that it was Flint and he now had a hope for light. He then took some more random stone and carved them into sharp pieces. Two sharp pieces were all it needed to get his work done. He cutted his overgrown hair from the back of his head and collected them in his hand. He too removed the T-Shirt and kept it down. There, he have enough hair to start a fire and so he tried, to succeed. He rubbed the flint stones together close to the hair and in minutes he acquired Fire. But he has to hurry cause the fire would go off soon. That's when he took the T-Shirt and made it catch fire, as he was just in time. Now the T-Shirt was burning and would go out of flames in minutes as the quality was good. He fast was hurrying to find something to keep on the fire when he came across it. A small natural shelter made by the stones coming ahead from top with space inside. The thing that was quite stunning, there stood a small hole, A size of watermelon with a strange liquid thing in it. The hole didn't looked natural and the small stones, were gathered in corner which made it possible that the hole was dug. He smelled the small quantity of liquid which was little bit like vinegar and he had a instant thought. But first he let the burning piece of T-Shirt in this liquid thing. It instantly burned, and Ajax guessed it. It was "acetic acid", also used in vinegar. But now the question arises, from where on earth did this thing came here. Before he could make his Theories, he recognized the time was running and there wasn't enough acid to keep the flames on. But, little did he know, his problems are going to be solved in a matter of minutes. He followed the undiscovered path of the cave and just by a little distance he saw what he described as a sword hunged up and reflecting light from it. But it was just an Old torch, An torch he said in a shook and excitement. Quickly removing the torch from it's stand on the wall he took it to the acidic flames. It burned, he now has torch with fire. He with his new torch now went through the path he found, to see about what he thinks. He found it and "Yes" it is it he said. 'No' not exactly. He found more three torch and he intended to burn them. There was real light now and he was able to see. "A Maze", There was a maze on the wall made of gold, now old and dusty with cracks on it, The old golden wall looked like the terminal of the cave. It was an Intresting maze but a hard one too. Determined to solve the maze as he has solved many before he said, "Here give way to the King of Maze solving". He took a good look on the Maze and after some seconds started to solve it using it's finger. HE failed and failed and failed But he didn't stopped trying, The maze was hard. It to was not the smallest one, with many ways but one to get through. So he decided to use his brain with as much concen to solve this thing. Ajax again failed and then many times more, But still trying, 'Some Determination'. It was now like 2PM and he has already spend more than 3hours in the cave. He was starting to want some food but there was this Maze to be solved. After he said this sentence this thought popped in his mind. "What is the point of solving this maze". He sat down and started to think, what should he do, this is the moment to chose the perfect thing to do cause a wrong step and it's all over. He then came to a conclusion, that this is the only hope. If I ignored the Maze, I will die but if I solve it There is chance to unlock the mysteries it holds, after some more effort and time. He solved the Maze. He was so excited to finally solve it, that he said it "Man, after this much of solving I remember all the ways". Ajax waited for something to happen as he has solved the maze, he called impossible to solve for amature solvers. "Nothing happened". Ajax felt grieved and thwart, but was convinced to have omitted something. He sat down hungrily and was thinking of the mistake his hurtled brain would have made in the process of maze solving. 'Huh', got it, why didn't before he said after 2minutes of thinking. He went back the way he came and picked up a sharp stone. Now in front of the Golden Maze he made a cut in his finger, in order to use his blood. He said, "This a blunder I made". He moved his finger towards the maze and with some glances. Started to solve the maze, now with his blood ink. It was his commen sense, that a maze is truly called solved when the path is highlighted by something. He quickly solved the maze with his blood as an ink. This proved that he remembered the paths. With his blood on the Maze he was aspirated to move ahead. He heard it a sound of something moving, and it happened. Ajax was seeing the Maze and the Golden Wall behind it moving. He saw some tiny stones falling beneath the maze. So he lay down on his stomach to see what was happening. Him starring at the tiny falling stones, was not able to figure out what was going to happen. The stones now almost stopped falling and the big carved stone on which the Maze was carved falled down. The Maze stone falled down enough to kill anyone standing in front of it. But it was attached to two chain strong enough to hold it. The Chain and the tiny falling stones just saved his Life. Ajax looked up and felt saved and lucky, he stood up, cleaning his clothes and backed off. Standing at a distance from the fallen maze. Suddenly the golden stone open like two wide golden doors. When the golden stone door almost opened completely it breaked into pieces. Ajax with a confused face was seeing all this happening but the thing that interest him was the tunnel behind the broken golden stone door. He without wasting any further thought stepped in the Tunnel. Walking in this circular path with the burning torch in his hands, he was again lost in thoughts. Some seconds of thinking and the tunnel came to an end where he could see it, The "Ancient Text". Ajax inspected the neither big nor small place and found. A circular outline in the stone wall above. It was small, of the size of a cars tire. He now knew the way of reaching this cave and the Ancient Text. But didn't know how to get out of it. So he tried to find a way out but found no clue. Which led him to check the outlined circle on the wall above. He knocked it between the outlined circle and heard a noise like it was empty the other side. He then went back the tunnel and took a piece of the broken golden door and came back to break it. "Smash" he broke the empty on other side outlined circle and saw "Light". There were ladder on one of the side of the new path to freedom from this dingy place. He started to climb and realized that these ladder where made of stone but how it was holding his weight? He being afraid that the ladders can break climbed up quickly and came out from where he started. The Tree he climbed, The Double Layered Leather Bag Of His, The Stone He Tripped And The Crash Of Nosorogs. He was stupefied of what just happened, 5hours it had been and he have discovered the Ancient Text with many surprises. He came out and sat down near his bag and fulfilled his wish of eating Food. He took his time munching on the food he had and the berries on the tree above his head as a sweet desert. Ajax now fresh and energetic decided to gather some woods. His plan:- First to gather woods for many uses like Making a Shelter for now, with strong defense, Making Fire and Block both the entries and exits of the sliding and climbing ways to the cave and The Ancient Text. He has enough food supplies to survive 3days but he decided to save the packed food for emergencies, that means to collect berries and fish. The next day after a good night sleep, he has to go explore the Ruins and the Island to know about it(gain information). All these things are some of the things responsible for his Future events. So he went up near the trees to gather wood in large quantity. "Huh" he said after reaching to a height, standing in the Mini forest. He brought his sword with him. "Yeaaah" first chop! and this goes forever. He chopped many wood and collected them to a place at the edge of this small forest near to where he was to make his shelter. It was almost dark and he was chilling, seeing the view of a Great Sunset on this Mystifying and Wonderful Island. He was coming down with his supplies of Wood tied to a rope he used before. He reached his place and a good thing The Nosorogs were not bothering him now. He tired from all his effort sat and removed his bottle of water, When he realized. "I will run out of my supplies of water in some days", Gotta work on this too he said. Okay now, so he used some leaves from the tree above and burned them using his lighter, then quickly burned the woods from the fire on the leaves, near his small camp. "Ajax now has proper Fire". He next used his sword and made small holes in the tree, 6feets in height from ground. The holes were made near 3cm from each other in the circular line of the Tree. The holes were not the deepest in the tree but deep enough to hold things in it. He then climbed up and brought the outer layer of tree (Bark) he peeled of before, he too bought some particular size of sticks. All this got him tired but he was a strong Man. Now The carpentry starts:- Ajax used his sword to make 7 sticks with sharp edged, one for each hole. He then used the back of his sword to make them stuck inside the holes made in the tree. After all the 7 sticks which he believes to be the strongest he picked were stuck inside he went ahead. Then he took the strong thread from his rope box he brought with many more thing and used it. By joining 4 sticks together in a line and make 14 pair like this. The sticks were big and he tied the threads at both the side (the beginning and the end). These 14 pair of 4 sticks tied together by a strong thread will be going to be his shelter. He used his another rope and tied it to the tree from one end with other end attached to his sword. Then he made a perfect circle on the upper layer of the soil, with the help of his rope and sword. He then took 7 broad branches almost of same size (6feet) from his collection of woods. sharpened only one of every edges and putted them in the earth, now more accurately because of the outlined circle. Then he used the leftover salt and stuffed it into the little gaps left in the holes where the sticks were strongly placed. After that he used the small Barks and placed them on the sticks connecting the tree. Then he placed the Big sticks on the Bark which was placed on the smaller stick. He then placed the other end of the first 4 sticks "tied together" to the 2 broader sticks of 6 feet or less placed in the earth. He did this 12 more times and all the sticks were placed in proper position. Then added the leftover Barks in the biggest gaps that can be see. With Leaves all over the Top, he Now Had a Brand New Shelter which he can call Home. Just one more thing and it will be more efficient he said. It was more than 8:00PM and he decided to dig a hole near the one with ladders. He didn't had a shovel so he used his Sword for this task too. He dug the hole deep enough with his sword and hand. "Now you would be wondering why did he did this (Dug a hole) there are 3 main reasons". First- to see if there is any other tunnel or some-kind-of thing hidden. Second- to burn wood for smoke, which will force the insects and bugs to leave the tree. Third- to make Charcoal from woods! He added many of the wood in the hole with some leaves he collected before and burn them to fire with some big sticks on top covering like a roof. He then took shade in his shelter and rewarded himself a nice dinner, breaking the second thing in his plan. He ate the food he had and some berries from the tree. "Yeah" many time the Nosorogs came near him but they were not his enemies and Ajax treated them well. After this dinner he took the ashes of the woods that were burning all the time and threw them on the top of the shelter. He to added some more wood to keep up the fire. After this tiring day he removed his sleeping bag and slept... The Night goes on but Ajax woke up early at 5:00AM. He is so used to it that he don't need any alarm to wake him up. "Morning Morning", he said to himself and started his 'warm ups'. After the 'warm ups' he did some exercise and running. He checked on the smoking Charcoal, which was looking good but he left it for some more time. Ajax played with the Nosorogs who were awake while he was running. He did these things till 6:30AM and then some peaceful rest. He lay down as he was tired and end up s-l-e-e-p-i-n-g. "Ahhh" A Good 2 hour Sleep he had and he was ready to go, after brushing. Ajax now removed his sword and started to move it in the air. Indeed he was practicing as he thought there was grave danger ahead. He did it for quite a while until he stopped. He sat down in the shades of the shelter and removed the book "Lamere". His Plan, to read the important information about the ruins before heading there himself. Ajax opened the Book Turned some Pages and:- "The Ruins of The Village, Pistós Miles". Pistós Miles is the name of the village, taken from 2 different language. The Queen who ruled the village and the people loyal to her named themselves "The People Of Vasílissa". The village was a great success in it's early years. 'Yeah' Pistós Miles before becoming a village was a kingdom, Ruled by A Queen "Maya Suki". The village was a peaceful place to live, people had enough space to live a life-of-luxury. The many houses made of stone were strong to sheild the people inside from strong wind currents and stormy weather. There where 95 to 105 houses when they were made, the number got reduced a little. The Village also consist of some monuments and many Great Structures for different things. The Beauty of the village was given by the brilliant people with their creative idea and The Magnificent Island. "The Island which happens to be the cause of its Extinction, leaving behind the Ruins for the ones who will ever know". There were 2 more Topics in The Book which should to considered "main", especially one of em. Ajax took his sword "SBA-GLADIUS-VESPARUM" and a bag he filled with "ropes, lighter, knife, electronic torch, water, packed food and berries, ect". 2 berries he ate and got on the way to the Ruins. A tiring half hour walk it was and he was remembring the story his grandfather told him when he was younger. The Story of the "Peoples Houses", his grandfather named. While Ajax was walking and seeing the alluring view towards the way to Ruins. He went inside his thoughts and remembered the story his grandfather told him. It all goes like this, Ajax a 8 year old kid sitting in the lap of his grandfather and Albert laying down with his favorite pillow as their grandfather says the story of the "Peoples Houses". "Five Men" there were, Strong and Adroit living in the Village. A Quirky one I must say. It was that old man again, he got chased by the those nasty big creatures. Who ended up destroying 3 houses, The people living their were usually calm and polite but this wasn't the first time their house were down in pieces. It had happened 3 times before this. (Albert asked So what did the 5 Men did) The Five Men used their strengths combined to make them people happy. The group of 5 with the talents of their own and The one Man with the Heart of a Lion with the abilities of a Leader, filled with courage and extraordinary power, he was talented and good in finding delightful solutions. ("Like you" Ajax asked) Yeah! he replied and added A Younger version of mine you can say. (Woow! These all things are goona help us so much, Albert said) Yeah! How? our old man asked. (tomorrow is literature test you see) The Old man was happy and he showed it with a laugh. Then he continued, Then that 1 Men out of 5 went to a place where many stones were found and some time later came with full energy. The Man we were talking about before brought a Tall Tree stem sharpened from both the side. Then Jumped putting it deep in the earth, all together then with their creative ideas build a brand new house. 2 days later they build houses for all the ones who have lost one. The interesting thing, The houses looked like a green mushroom with broader stem and a window. This story increased Alberts imaginations power (That's what any story is meant for!!!) and fascinated

Ajax. This story was the one Ajax was thinking on the way to the village. Ajax was trying to remove some kind of meaning of it. Anyways, here he was "standing right front of the village where once stood an Empire!". He wearing a bag and a sword in his hand moved ahead. The view of this Ruins was 1 in 1,000,000,000 But to Ajax it was breathtaking. He saw the ruins from long distance and now standing in front of it made him emotional. Just some tears from his crying eyes and an other story going in his Mind. He controlled his feelings, took a long breathe and wiped his tears. Then with a graceful move from his sword "Fast and Strong", putting it deep in the earth. Ajax kneel down both of his legs and bowed down his head holding the sword and showed his Respect. He said "I know I may do it and I will, I will!" He stood up like a warrior with his Reddish eyes and removed The sword from the ground. His eyes were full of tears as he walked in The Old Village. Pistós Miles a great village why has it to be destroyed, he asked himself. He saw many monuments and Houses some were a flat place now hard used for some purpose, a circle empty from inside with one entry as it was used for storage, a staircase going to a height of 11feet with no part of it not even brocken pieces and a flat stone in the air supported by 4 metal sticks. As he was looking for some clue or the things that would be left by the "The People Of Vasílissa" or the villagers. That was when he came across the Tower, A tower said to be Great and Tall but only 2 brocken floors left now. He too saw a stair with no other structure on the Right and a rock plate with 4 rods supporting it on the Left. The moment, when he was going to step inside it, that he showed up.

CHAPTER THREE

The Immortal Past to a Magical Future

It was Sthenarós Milos. The Beast looked terrifyingly angry and Ajax only saw one of them, making him more agitated. The one alone would be impenetrable, for him to do his work. Milos there tried to stare in Ajaxs eyes causing him to make his Mane stand(Manes are the fur around the face, like lions Mane). Sthenarós looked him in his Red eyes trying to manipulate him. But his eyes were bloody red and hard to manipulate. Ajax slowly moved ahead and gave out a weird scream, which, somehow made the Beast back-of. He was trying to go near him so that he could calm it or if not, "Make his sword bloody". He came ahead as milos was not reacting, he moved his right hand close, trying to comfort. The Beast, as his hand comes closer was like freezed with his Big eyes looking at him. When he was to touch, it reacted violently. Ajax knew this was a possibility so he stepped back and came ahead to Hurt it. This play went on for sometime and they were fighting and changing their position all over in the village. It was the moment finally, "both tired and standing at a distance" when. He moved ahead going for the legs. "sthenarós Milos" was no less, it came ahead without fear and his hard head. Strongly pushing him back. By luck should I say? The sword just missed the Head. Ajax fell down on a distance close to the structure where he could have "Bumped" his head. He tried to stood up with his bloody eyes, to get his fallen sword. Milos saw that and ran for him when Ajax jumped up without any weapon but a damaged bag on his back. It pushed him again and now forcing him to fall in the dried "well" behind. He fell deep and was alive because of it's slide type structure but he was fainted. 2minutes later nothing happened. "Clint" a sound came and something hard hit his stomach. He woke up, in a "place darker than any light". He described it as some light was present in the well but it was to Dark to be seen. He stepped on something, which happens to be his sword. He picked it up, looked at it and ran at full speed. Towards the entrance of the place he entered by mistakenly and he saw the face of sthenarós looking for him but the moment it saw him milos ran away. There was light coming from the top of the well but very less. And turning back, seeing to the dark side of the inside of the dried well he was agitated. Ajax removed the torch from his bag, he turned it on and saw a path, a small in length tunnel. The early people would be erudite and skilled to make this tunnel, he said. The tunnel was going straight down and then it suddenly took a turn becoming a very small slide, then after it ended, the slide, it was a straight path of only 12 to 18m made of stone. Now as he don't have many-things to do but to escape alive, he had some ideas. He quickly removed the long and strong wide rope from the bag, then tied 3 knots from one end. He could now use the rope for multiple purpose. The well was deep(120feet) and the rope could not reach the top but by using his brain he could still escape. But, he has his own plans, he wanted to check this suspicious little place. So he removed his plastic bottle of water which was bent a little from the bottom and drank much of it. Then placed the torch in the bottle to make a small DIY lamp. Now he could see more efficiently. The rope, he used it to hit the walls of the well by standing mostly in a place, rotating the rope to see for weak points by their sound. He with full power and speed threw the rope randomly as the top was hard because of the knots. He didn't achieve much success. But the sound when the rope hit the wall was different and empty some times. He anyway just wanted to get out and come here again later but that's the thing. He had no clue how to get out of this dry well. He was thinking an idea to get out of this place and at the same time finding a hole or a weak point in the wall. It's been an hour and he has found some weak points in the wall but was afraid there can be anything behind. The well was situated from a distance away from Pistós Miles. He decided to break the weak points in the well as he could not find anything else to do and so he did. He used the back of his sword and smashed it into the wall breaking a portion of it. The thing he found was that the wall had a very small path, smaller that his body going somewhere after the turn from some distance. He broke all the weak point he found and all had the same thing, a path taking a turn. All the places he break were like making a pattern. He now had some stones, which he was thinking would be of some use when something popped in his mind. The corners "Yes", the corners is the best place to make a way behind, he said. Then with the stones, he started to break the corners. It wasn't to hard, the wall breaked and he was right the weak points he breaked before were a distraction. But a distraction for what? he asked himself. He thought if there were any weak points, corners are the best place to make him. By this the chances increase to it not to be found, as not everybody check corners for this purpose. He squeezed himself through the hole with sharp edges, he just breaked(the corners he breaked). and there he was standing with some cuts in his arms. He saw a carved, big and heavy stone, blocking the way ahead. He had his torch yet, so he was searching for a clue to move ahead. He punched the stone and here, 'hand pain', he too tried to push, fall or break it with other things he could find, but failed. There was this one thing, whenever he hit the carved stone, he could feel something to slight to be noticed. He hitted it countless number of time, until this happened. The last time he had to hit the stone, he hitted it so hard that it collapsed. Which caused a vibration he could feel, it cracked the ground beneath and breaked a part of itself. Ajax moved ahead and found Great Treasure hidden by the Queen. A treasure containing Gold, Emralds, Gems, Diamond and Many Many More. He was happy to see this but was not intreasted in it. The thing that he wanted was to escape this place. He went back to bring his bag and on the way noticed something suspicious about the fallen stone. But "Nothing is greater than Hunger" and with the desire to eat he went ahead. He reached back, eating some food he had and the bag which was almost empty, he filled it with all the treasure he can fit. He after scrutiny found this a different way, going up, he investigated the way. Which happens to be a ZigZag path to freedom, however when he climbed up he saw spikes. Spikes thin and pointy from top and wide and strong from bottom. He in his mind got an idea. He made a oval from the top of his rope by tied a knot. This way(path) was made out of concrete and he was expecting some traps to be there, blocking the path. Ajax warmed-him-up and went ahead to get out of this place. In the ZigZag path he threw the rope in the spike from a near distance. Then climbed up, now with the support of the rope tied to the spike. He was up in the first level and him not being fat was able to pass from the gap in the side of the spike. He kept climbing up with his rope and taking advantage of the sharp spikes. Until it happened, Ajax knew something like this was going to happen. The problem was the number of spikes increased but there was some space for him to pass through. He struggled to move ahead, hurting his body mostly because of the spikes. And then on a level high, after climbing many zigzag levels, The path was blocked by many spikes, it was impossible to get through. He now had 2 choice to get back or break through and the thing that makes the second option more risky was he had no idea what was ahead. He choosed the second option with a plan to break the top of the spike so that he could break the others(spikes) from it. All to the power of this strong hand he said. Then moved his hand in full speed which missed the aim causing the top of the spike to tear a layer of his skin of the hand. "Ahhhh" he screamed but still determined to move ahead. He did what he planed but his hands were literally destroyed. He moved ahead as he destroyed the spike and his hand, where the things get more complicated. he climbed 2 levels without any spikes and then found another set of spike pointing in all direction. He was feeling aggrieved already and these sets of incident made him frustated. He noticed one thing There was no concrete on the top of the many spikes, instead there was dirt. He took his sword and started to remove the dirt, to make space for him to pass through. He did it and now was ready to go ahead. The path was like a straight slide and the spikes were a trap, so people coming down would die or hurt themselves by the spikes if not noticed it. A trap to save the treasure. He got out climbing the dirt slide and saw light, Light from the Sun. There were carved stone and flowers growing from where he came out. It was like he was standing on a graveyard but it was different. He saw something moving, behind the tree. He assumed it to be an animal or something but there was no reason for it to not be a Human. He unlike many others went to scrutinize that what was the case. he went in the woods looking for that figure and the only things he had was his Sword, Rope and a bag filled with some expensive stuff. He searched for sometime but was not-able to find anything. The news was, Ajax was lost "A wrong move and that’s all it takes" came in his mind. And he knew he had done a big mistake. He was standing in "The Wood of Hantu", The good thing he was not in the middle of the forest but in the side near The Volcano. So the most reasonable thing to do according to him was to head for the top of the volcano. As the mountain could be seen and it was high, so he could find his new shelter and home. There is a Great History of The Mountains too. It is known to be a Dormant volcano. He headed towards it and was gleeful from inside. He ran in brimful speed, thinking about the pleasure he was going to get. 5minutes that’s all it took for him to reach the mountain, But now he has to climb up. Yeah and that took a pair of hour, and he was there to his destination. He enjoyed the tranquil effect on reaching the destination. The thing he saw was "Hot Springs". It was bewitching and he almost want to dip in, "Yeah" almost. The thing that fascinated him more was "Sulphur".

He gave a strong smile and breaked the sulphur crystal using his sword. He was auspicious and delighted that he could not control his happiness. He was feeling strong and used that limited feeling of supernatural strength to collect as much sulphur as he could as soon as possible. He did it till it was night, ("Yep" the feeling ended when the work came in), and then he took the gratification of the Hot spring. (Just so you know Ajax always liked the dip in the hot spring and he hadn't taken one from a very long time, until now) He was in for like almost 2 hours. When he could not take anymore, 'his hunger', he was hungry from hours. So he decided to go back home. He reached home with his sulphur which he kept in the bag and transferred the part of the treasure in another bag he made from his rope. There he saw an Arrow with a letter. He was dazed and couldn't stop wondering who could have send him this in a island no one can enter, Then. "Up Above He Saw He crouched". He found nothing but the view of the dark sky. He opened the letter and couldn't read anything as there was nothing written in it. He with an eerie feeling saved the letter by putting it to a safe place and drank fresh water he bought. Having 2 places, useful and important to investigate further, he read about them in the book of Lareme. First about the treasure he searched in it's relating criteria and found nothing but this:- "A Treasure one cannot imagine deep in the bore Adam's ale" He was confused and not much in it as he already has found the treasure. Turning some pages he found about this interesting thing(according to him). About a thing that used to be popular among everybody. A Graveyard unutterable and cryptical to the villagers. It is beleived that The Graveyard, it's it local name, Is a place where horrible things were done to people by THEM. They would burry people Alive in the magical grounds when they do things not to be done. The Graveyard is a place where no one comes alive if entered deliberately or mistakenly. The souls of 47 people are still known to be alive in the form of energy and waiting wretchedly for a victim for blood. "The People Of Vasílissa" are very afraid of this place, everybody is, and wouldn't dare to go near it. The place was traped in a invisible, a circle made to cover the place, to keep everybody safe. The place shouldn't be visited, is not seen by any eye, 'The circle' but entering it would disable the sheild and the person would no longer be safe. Ajax after reading this was frustrated and worried and was anxiously thinking where the place would be. He let it go and was starting to feel sleepy but still want to read some information given in the book. He then read about the Ancient Text. A message passed on for generation in the form of Text. The knowledge of the Unknown and

The clue for The Future. The Information of The Great and The Secreat of the Island. A Text to the key, hidden in a place normal to see. "Ancient Text" the most valuable and important peice for the Fall and the Rise of the mysteries lying ahead. Rather bit of confused he was but was ready for the challange waiting ahead. He took rest and went to sleep. Dreaming about things so wonderful that it makes its hard to explain. Waked up after a good night sleep he was fresh and ready to go. So he cleared all the minor work and had a thought, "Were to go". He had a long complicated thought and decided to go from the slide behind his home to The Ancient Text, he stood up and. There he saw a man falling the same way he was in the depths of the menacing cave. He went for saving him and hold his hands to prevent him from falling. He lifted him up and made him sit, and asked who-how are you. The man looked up and Ajax was stunned and astonished, "Albert!" he said. "Yeah!" it's me brother thanks for helping. Yeah, off of-course, But how did you falled, in the first place? Ahh just a stupid stone I guess, he replied. A lively conversation in Exhaustence. You made this he asked while seeing the shelter of his brother, You copied much of my idea in it. No I learned it from myself. But how did you came here and like just how. Well I just made a telepoter he replied in exuberance. No you can't you can't, how did you do it, asked with enliven. No you dum oaf I can't make one and teleport here with or without a teleporter. Hooouww! See I would need a machine here to teleport to here and I just so happens to have magical power riiight and you should know after being on this island for a decade that humanity havn't made a teleporting machine yet, he said. Chill out big bro and act like yourself, tell me how did you came here? "Hemmhh", with a small giggly laugh he said (with loud voice) "Science, science has a way to defeat all the danger and challenge nature or some power can ever present to stop me." With big eyes Ajax replied that's like you and you better calm down cause I have many things to show you. Yeah yeah Albert replied and sat down. Then after 2minutes Albert asked 'now tell me everything you have gained information off' and one more thing! "Did you found him!" No!!! he replied sadly and with a pause said, you shouldn't have told that. You have to except the truth! Albert shouted and then asked for everything he has done. Ajax started to tell him everything but something was wrong. He told Albert everything except somethings he wanted to keep to himself. Albert being like a boss instructed Ajax to go up to the woods and do this work. He gave him some things that will be useful to him and made him go. Ajax switched his sword with another one, the one with magical power and known to be the strongest of its kind. Ajax with many things including charcoal went up with the intension to bring woods and clean water. He climbed up and took a rest thinking about, The figure he saw, The Sthenarós and the other beasts with all the things he had done after coming to this island with the intent to detect the clue left behind. He knock down many dead trees after purifying the water with charcoal. Then... In the middle of cutting of tree he saw it again! A green light forming a figure, he knew it was the thing that can be called "Magic!". He walked towards it with his sword and as you would or wouldn't have expected, it was running away. He chased it but it was fast, so he threw a stone he picked up from down and saw it didn't went through it. That means it was something other than a ghost, something more alive. He followed it at an unbelievable speed and took a jump ahead of it striking it with his sword. It split into two but joined again, then something unexpected happened. It all got absorbed in his sword, his sword started to glow green after it and he could not waste a minute. He gathered the wood and the water in a bag his elder brother gave and with the sword he rushed to him. He reached their falling and hasting to his brother who was trying to figure out the riddle. Ajax said you have to see it. "It is true". Grandfather! he is still alive, he has been for all this time! and he is here! I felt it! Albert replied, Why 'It is glowing' wait! how can you? what is this? See this green magical light it was floating and moving I saw it. You see this is some kind of Magic I know I felt it and we both know what he said. He can't be this and you don't know what it is and you like how and why did you brought it here Albert said? Remember Albert remember he told us and you know who our Grandfather is he belonged here and I happens to be the one who can feel it and I did! brother he is gone, and throw it away Albert told and threw the sword. Just after the sword fell it started to move and something a Monster in green started to come out. This is our grandfather now you see! It was there the Monster and was going to attack them when somebody came for the rescue. A Man with a trimmed beard, brown hair, cyan eyes and a strong body! He came from nowhere and slapped his hands together creating a Magical power! The monster vanished in thin air. Then he saw back making the brothers stupefied, Ajax asked, How are you! as Albert looks his face. There is no time for it. You both have to come with me! he said it and grabbed there T-shirts, teleporting them to a place Dark and Magical. They were there and still in shock when Ajax asked you know this all, Don't you! he asked to Albert. No! how! Teleportation you see Ajax replied. No it was just an freaking joke which came real I don't know how.

Ajax asked, I don't know how but I think I am familier with this guy! Your stupid hallucination, but if I come to think of it I am to, was his reply. Stop talking you both the man instructed in a familier way while looking behind. The place where everybody currently is. Was dark, disturbing and somewhat royal on it's own. There was a throne and lave flowing from a side, which in front of the man was standing. The place looked ancient made with black hot rocks, a platform where they were standing. A stick made of tungsten with many great features and magical powers came from the lava flowing and he grabbed it and walked towards the throne. He then sat like a king holding his stick and said. "The honor of yours that you are standing in front of the King of the Island!!!" Or I should say "The Honor is all Mine!" I so happens to be you boths Grandfather! What Albert said while Ajax was stunned. It was a seconds pause and then Ajax moved ahead and said "A fleeting death for a persistent living!!!" "A fleeting death for a persistent living!!!", he replied backed. Why? What happened?? and why not us??? Albert asked. You were too young and this place wasn't safe for you both as both of you are the one with the Magic in a high aggregate. But how did you lived and what about the new look? Well you know I happens to be a citizen of this village maybe the only one alive and now happens to be "The King of This whole Island!" But Grandfather we have lot of things to solve and many things to do, to explore... No time, there is a big problem very big. She is back with her powers greater than any of us he said while looking in Ajaxs eyes. We can't grandfather you are telling the wrong thing, we must go according to the poem-riddle we have already done a mistake coming to "Nekrós Lieweg". He then moved ahead and teleported with both of them and took them to the shelter he made. "Rest", both of you, tommorow is the day, till then rest. But grandfather that lightening ("his grandfather opened his eyes big") that we thought you were no more. Some magical power aye, not the most powerful for no reason, he replied. He saw Ajaxs hand and asked did you gave your blood to anybody? No he replied. Ok off you go to sleep. Albert was reading Lamere and about the riddles while Ajax was making something with the resources available he had a way to make something called "Gunpowder". He had two important ingredients already, Sulphur and charcoal, but he still needed Potassium nitrate (KNO3). And it seems like he has a way for it, to ask his brother. who gave him 3 option and he had to chose the 1st one as he don't have any other choice. It so seems that Albert happens to have Potassium hydroxide in a form and they only need to find ammonium nitrate. Which they extracted from an icepacks Ajax had, then after mixing both together and making fine powder out of it. The only thing left was to mix charcoal, sulphur and potassium nitrate into fine powder. And they did it, Ajax finally made Blackpowder or Gunpowder. He made 3kg of it and saved it for later, It is going to play a big role in the future said Albert, 'Yeah' I know Ajax replied. As there grandfather was gone Albert invited Ajax to have a seat with him in the shelter Ajax made. They both sat under the shades of it with their heads out looking at the Night Sky. 3days it's been, you are gone to fulfill your desire with the mission of your own, and I have no clue for you are alive. "Huh", Yeah I was worried for you, can't let you die! Ajax closed his eyes as Albert continues, Things dosn't seem like it is and so do I! I knew he could be alive, his inspiring quotes! I could never forget it and I always knew he was, alive... Ajax started to cry and said 10years... It is a long time and after that he proved everybody wrong and his lines live. But he has changed not just by his looks. Albert said, We shall not forget who we are, you know it's a blessing, that we are Magical. An island where it was born and it runs in our veins. They both slept after some talks and his last sentence was "We should not forget Grandmother too". They woke up by a loud noise and say everything was fine. It was already morning and they had waked up properly now. So where is it? Albert asked, what? Ajax asked to Albert. The Danger and our immortal grandfather, he said tommorow is the day. After this sentence he appeared, their grandfather and said "I told you tomorrow is the day, the day to rest". What!! are you serious we have an 'enemy' that can destroy the whole island in seconds and what are you telling ,rest! Albert said angrily. Yeah that's what you will do both of you old man replied with a little high voice. Albert with deep exhales and inhales said "You have no idea how I came here" and after saying this he ran towards the buildings to run for the woods of "Hantu". Ajax followed him but his grandfather stopped him and with a still and confused face and eyes looking in his, then teleported. This should not have happened he said and wanted to go after his big brother, but. The voice stopped him, The voice inside stopped him. He took a cup of tea he stored earlier, to calm him down. While he was drinking he just said 2 words to himself, two words enough to bring tears in his eyes. The words were "It's okay" and he had a flashback, seeing his brother and grandfather saying him "it's okay" all the times in their lifetime to him. When he was weak, when he was stucked, when he was alone and when he was a step away. He stopped and closed his eyes, sitting in medatative position and the thing happened! That could prove "he is worthy". He was starting to go in the "Deep Thought". "Deep Thought an incredible stage of going inside your mind which connects the 3 main parts of existence." Ajax was in "deep thought" imagining the things shown by a strong source of "Eternity", a magical connection between him and eternity directly. A painful method which would kill if not from one who can take it. He was in very pain screaming "Ahhhhh" when he stopped, like he was dead. Ajax was seeing The moment he had lived, seeing him as younger and living the magical moment again as a kid, teen and adult. He was seeing this all with the flash of him in the present time sitting with his legs fold and eyes closed. Then this started to come, the things never has he seen before. It was a mixer of memory the one he had lived, the one living and the one to come! The sceneries, views and things never seen before are placed like this. The scenery of the island "Nekrós Lieweg" but different, Nekrós Lieweg was filled with people, who happens to be dancing in a very traditional and perfect way. The people were looking furious and not the most happy, it was very early morning, there was 3hours or so for the sun to rise. The scene then changed after a zoom into the moving picture. The next thing he has never seen was A women sitting on a the throne and the family of three standing in front of her as their grandfather knees down. Their were magical lights and lightening of green and blue all over. The women on the throne moves her red stick and hits it in the ground making a high force and the scene sifted. Then the next one was Him sitting on the brocken building, He was sitting on the great tower on the small place on the top and his brother and grandfather on both his sides. They were looking like they were dead and the one beside him were their spirits. It was a very quite moment compared to others. He thought they were flying when thcy were standing on the edge of the rocks that's when they jumps down and the second later he fades away in dark pink light, it was night again. It changed and comes to the final view after many memories of the past. He sees many animals, birds and even big fish in anger and eyes red. They were all running, flying and swimming in the lead of "The Women from the Throne". They were all looking like they were in a fight or should I say a "War". Then the scene continued to a big blue-yellow lightening and light, something inside was leading the lightening as a "God". These were all the things he has never seen before and the memory of him throughout his life he had lived. He was levitating in real life and was seeing that too what was going on with him in the form of flashes in his Deep Thought. He also saw every danger he has faced related to the island and the legend. His grandfather arrived their(teleported there) with Albert and was seeing what was going on with Ajax. Ajax was in middle of experiencing what was going on with him when they both arrived. The weather started to change and a Thunderstorm was coming. It wasn't late as it started to rain and lightening falled all over the island. It all ended(the Deep Thought) and the thunderstorm started to gain power. Ajax fell down, the levitation ended and he opened his eyes. Grand he said faintly, his grandfather helped him stand up and some seconds later he was in consciousness again. He started to say what happened as Albert was watching him with big eyes. His grandfather stopped him and said there are other ways I can know faster, and touched his index finger to Ajax head. A mistake he did and was thrown meters behind by the strong force. Ajax was in extreme pain lying in the hands of his grandfather when he came back, losing consciousness again. "It was the sound of silence in his ears, his vision started to get blurry as if he was going blind and he was experiencing shortness of breath. He screamed in pain not able to describe it was faith or unfortunate that he was still alive to feel the pain. But, He fainted in the hands of his grandfather as he(his grandfather) was worried he wasn't gonna make it but Albert was seeing something he wasn't... The sight Albert was seeing was paramount, significant, extraordinary, exceptional rare and never to be seen before and maybe ultimate. Albert with his own eyes alone was seeing Ajax covered in scorching Fire, safeguarding Water, layer of Rocks orbiting him representing Earth and Rainbow light(Magical energy) which flows in the Air of the island, flowing all around himself. This was a sight only Albert can see, only him.

CHAPTER FOUR

The Trio for the Go

Noo! We should go from here, he is dying, old man said. Wait "He is not", Albert announced. He is the master of all and he is strong, he is not dying. I see it. His grandfather looked in his eyes and believed him leaving Ajax in the home he made and asking what to do next to Albert. With a deep breath he said "Wait!", and think, we have to, no choice. The Thunderstorm is coming close we have to go to a place well protected, Albert asked. And I just so happens to know one he replied. He then teleported to a place bright and white with both his grandsons. It was a room somewhere in the island which looked modern. There was a bed where Ajax rested, It was night when Ajax woke up but the day, it was just as dark as night. They both rushed to him and Ajax let them know everything he saw. It was cleared to him now about the "Deep thought" when his grandfather told him. 'Deep Thought' a term used to frame the knowledge that joins Space and Time. A thing exceptionally rare for anybody, Any from any who has the honor will be great even if not. The things seen in the process connected to the concept of Time. The pain to be survived, the suffering to be taken, would alone be able to kill them all. It's a blessing to be lived the agonization and a duty to fullfil everything and add to the story. Yeah it was written in Lareme. It was very important and helpful especially at this moment. His grandfather asked about the women and to describe her more. The women was full black, black eyes, black hair (as he described her old man got more nervous)and black clothes which doesn't looked from our modern world, it was time then her this color was for some time when it changed into blonde only her skin. The thing to worry the most "She looked Magical" he said. Their grandfather was feeling nothing, he was in his own shock. When he said "She is back", who? Albert asked. Old man replied The one who was the greatest, "The 2rd Royal Queen of our Great Dynasty", who happens to be the last but now she will rise again a Ruler to rule them all. Calm down grandfather it's not just about her, think for yourself you too Albert said . I saw you-both, it was your last moment and I-was-there, Ajax concluded. Everybody took a break an lay down in order to rest and recover when after some time Ajax asked where are we... A bright cyan light flashed which was the light of them 3 teleporting to shelter made by Ajax and it was the next day. It looks like they slept good for hours after bringing Ajax to that bright place as it was 2PM. So now what to do Albert asked, I have to go, it looks like I have found something Old man let them know and went. I know what to do! We shall go according to the book, it's a hope and we have to survive at least till it's time!!! Ajax replied to Alberts question. He then removed the book and It opened on its own to the page where the poem was located and read itself...

The use, "Double", for that left behind
The Concotion and Raging of-the-mind
As to get Acquaint of the Regal bygone
And the Escalation of Loyalty long ago has gone
Conjunction together the Magic it shows
To open the thing, To open the Door
The Mentle wars and the brainwash above
The thing they hate, The things they Love
The Volcano with the Lava it possess
The sacred place, 'blistering', as its address

They both looked each other and Ajax courageously said Come on we should go, Yeah yeah and stop acting like a kid we have read it before, he replied. Yeah but I found something he told and with his sword went for the top. They were racing to the top of the mountain and where almost there when. "Wait" he said, The poem it has, That means, Albert while thinking said, "Yes" Ajax replied in excitement, "No" not just one, it can mean two things. I have to go, wait Ajax asked and told remembered "Peoples houses". Albert got another of his clue and with a brave-strong smile moved towards the Ruins. While Ajax removed his sword, Magical one, and moved it round, and the air responded like he was controlling it. Then with a deep breathe threw it in the volcano in which he by mistakenly cut his palm a little making it bleed. He saw the moment as the sword goes down in the lava, he had hope something will happen so he waited. He waited and cleaned the wound by his T-shirt, nothing happened to the sword. He lost it he felt and there was no sign of it. He sadly and fearful of what they both will say returned to the shelter he made. When, there was yellow lightening coming from the dormant volcano, it isn't sure it was lightening but it looked like.

There too were many light(energy) and strong flow of magical air coming from it. He missed it he was almost 50m away from it thinking and he missed it. He just kept moving ahead until he reached his destination, then lay down and was lost in thought. He was just about to sleep when he opened his eyes wide open and screamed to himself "wake up!". His brain was going infuriate and yeah he was feeling that he is losing his marbles. He without any second thought went down the stone staire to the Ancient Text. He didn't knew what to do, so in anger he breaked all the Texts from where it was attached to(the wall). His plan was to bring them all out but the space was very small. In his madness he saw small gold blocks, located just behind the place where the Texts rested for centuries. He collected all 4 of them and being small enough to fit in his palm, he thought from the leftover ration part of his mind which was still active. That he should bring those out and keep the Text down for now. He came out climbing the staire or ladder and skipped a beat of his heart when he saw behind. It was his grandfather starring at him strict and standing straight looking at him with a serious and ghostly looking face. He invited Ajax to a place he has never visited before located on Nekrós Lieweg". He moved his hand ahead and said 'with it', Ajax hold his hand firmly and they both teleported. They reached their, to the back of the island and were standing on a cliff. Old man said with hand spreading wide "remember this place son we 'are' going to come back here again." Then he took his hand teleported him to a place completely dark with no sign of light (till now). He asked Ajax remember something?! Do you?! Grandfather started to hear deep breathing made by Ajax. His heart started to pump fast and he was so nervous and anxious, I memory never to be forgotten. Overcome it, you are not weak! old man said, but it was not working. He realized(his grandfather) that now is the perfect time and did it. He went ahead and lift the purple stone up which then started to glow. At that moment he kept it down again and got aside. The light was so much that it filled the room with purple color and then... Everything changed! Light started to come out of the stone like it comes from a projector and he saw some visions from the past. They saw:- He first saw a man Old but Young sitting on a throne with his stick and he was talking to some people ordinary but great if compared to. Then in the next scene he saw A book which everybody now is familiar with, lying a table and the old-young man we saw before in front of it. He was making a spell using magic and not just spells but a charms, an hex, an enchantments or a bewitchery and something special. Something different in a magical way, something from that which everybody have, something given by a creator He-believed. A type of energy it means and he made all these and many more in his lifespan. Then the scene switched on this one when he with his army and many of the animals from the island was in a war against a dangerous, creepy and weird looking man with his army. Ajax saw some sight of the fight and our old-young man winning. Soon after seeing some views he saw old-young man dying somewhere he didn't know on the island. Then He saw another one, Queen of the island which was in the magical clips of the old-young King. "She is his daughter", his grandfather let him know. He saw her sitting on the same throne too in the palace and yes with her stick. After some viewing of the minor things like seeing her with her small kid. Then next main one was the Queen who was controlling fire and water together in a place looking like a cave for something important, she was the 2nd ruler of the Island. The last clip he saw was the Queen getting hit by a familier looking sword right in her stomach. It was her last moment as her eyes got closed forever. There was a face you will be familiar with now not far away from where the incident took place. The next ruler of the island The man with medium long brown color beard. sitting on the thron with his brown stick and looking in someones eyes like an ambitious king. The next major scene, him dancing with his axe like he has experience in that dance. Just a scene later we see the king going to a fight with almost a 10,400 creatures alone and the thing to be astonished is he won the dense fight, he was the 3rd ruler of the island. Ajax then saw him with his daughter, the great daughter, he was talking to her before going to a war. The last scene about him was him standing in front of another evil great man, both holding 2 sword and stopping each others hands to kill the other. Sadly at last the other man stabbed his one sword in his leg and the other one right in his heart. But our King was not-at-all weak, he moved ahead, threw the sword in his left hand up which got the other mens attention and that's when he cut off his head. He won the war and died a death of the most bravest. The era changed and a new one came, It was the Rise of Maya Suki. He saw the memory of her when she was 16 with her skin color changing to white, he saw her looking some portraits of all the rulers in general and her father in specific. The thing to be glad, he saw the memory going in her head, she was imagining every king and queen and the great things they did and, it was just the other day to the death of the Greatest King and her father, his grandfather was stunned. The scene changed to another major one. She was 'yes' sitting in the throne her father once sat, she was holding a stick of her own and stood up as the tears come down the eyes. The scene changed now seeing her in a room with burning candle the only source of light. She was doing some kind of ritual, holding a special liquid in a glass flask in her hand, she poured it in a very special transparent and holy liquid in a stone bowl lift by another stone block little bigger than a tier. It was like the scene was skipped as it sifted to the end of the ritual, she make a cut in her palm and sacrificed her blood, then put her face in it and the scene changed. Now to another one she was with the locals and the island was looking different from the current time. She was listening to the local talks by the locals when a monster attacked. She being a queen came ahead to save the day. Fire coming out of her hands she made a fireball officially starting the fight. The fight went for hours and she end up killing the monster never defeated before. The memory changed to one before the war, she was shining her weapons before going to a war which was the biggest one in the Magical history of the islands. She was up and in front of her stood the strongest and the dangerous Man in their history. It was a fierce fight and the longest one too, it was there to the most emotional end, that's all Ajax could see. She was holding the sword given by her father in front of the merciless enemy. He was stabbed by at least 15 sword many arrows and the most painful wounds but he was still alive with no strenght left but an intension to kill Maya Suki. She walked ahead close to him, and when she was close enough he removed a sword and stabbed it right in her shoulder. It didn't affected her though, she moved ahead and cut the bloody head off his body just like her father. Then after this scene he saw the island as before with a glich of it as now. Soon it came, he saw the island vanishing in dust with rainbow colors but darker. The tour through past ended and the room slowly became dark as the purple light faded away. They could see now as his grandfather glinted the room with big wide flamy torch. Reason!? Why did you showed me this? and why not Al? he asked politely. He has already seen it! and it is important for you to know! he replied wisely. Who are you? Do you know, what is going to happen? Ajax asked with some sadness on his face. Huh, You will know! he replied and moved his hand ahead and said it is already 6:30. He looked in his eyes moved his hand ahead and the both teleported to the cliff they came before. They view was great, the view of the sunset it was truely A sight to prepossessing to forget. They sat there and talked about their family and stuff in the shadows of the greatest island Nekrós Lieweg. The sky was maroon and the water was reflecting the view, there were creatures in water, air and ground. I can assure you this, Ajax can never forget this view, making him strong in the times of the true knowledge. The sun was down and they moved to the shelter by walking politely, more of quite than talks. There when they were almost there to the Ajax shelter both of them saw Albert with ripped clothes which looked like was formed by somebodies attack. 'Urggh' was Ajax reaction, it didn't bothered Albert anyway. He stood up and told them something big, something he achieved which almost killed him and took alot of time. He showed them up and the thing was extraordinary enough to pop their head. It was The Axe. The Axe of the Greastest king, The father of the Greastest Queen. He found it the Axe of the 3rd Ruler, it was beleived to be hidden and to be kept hidden until the perfect time. He was able to pick it, and somehow knew where to find it. He showed them a glass circle, a glass ball with the colourful statue of the Island in it. And the final thing, a stone 7cm in height with carvings on its back, there was written. "4 4 inside you find it". His grandfather was so impressed he told them, It's time to show you both my personal work-house, don't mind I call it that. Hmm was Ajaxs reaction and Albert told Now! Come one it's a good place and I bet you are gonna like it. They teleported after that and came to a place looking ancient, there were tables, chairs beds and many more, there was alot of space. And that was not it there was a second room attached with 2 long table and many more stuff on and around. "Wow" you lived here for the past 10 years?! No! things just kept upgrading. Come to the point the riddle what are the things left to find meaning on and work on it, Albert asked. "We can never find everything sons!" "My greatest longing will be fulfilled if, never", Old man told with his index fingure pointing up. These things why they have to be in the form of riddles? Ajax asked. Cause they test for the person or group if they are worthy was the reply. They spend there hours with the intension to find something as the thing not mentioned yet and Albert changed his clothes. No suspense! It is, "Anybody who attempts to get an answers of the riddles for a reason reasonable will be hexed to think in complicated ways and often be confused and sometimes start forgetting things about or relating to it." There was this thing they know, something about the stick. They conjectured that a stick by a particular discrete Ruler would be able to control many sorts of things and creatures. That reminds me from where and whom did you got your stick grands? This is very special, I got it from The Greatest Queen herself she gave me this with some words to be remembered he told with satisfaction. So give me your stick grands there can, Noo this is not supposed to be given to anybody and dosn't possess any power like that, said with some loud voice. Okay I guess so some other one he said. We should go for what we have instead of wasting time here plus we both have gained a lots and lots of knowledge while being here! You have a point but we shall go for our hunt tommorow. Yeah kids I have some extra beds old man said. Whooh you have more than 3beds Ajax said, Stop calling us kids we are grown-ups now Albert said. They went to sleep after that and before, they decided to wake up at 7AM...

ΔΔΔ

A new day it was and they woke up some minutes early to 7AM without any alarm. They got ready till 7AM and the first question Albert asked him in whispers, is the brown bag safe!!! Of course bro it is safe. Good, so a new day Sun is up our grands is sleeping and we have some heavy duty on our shoulders, Albert told, asked and looked in his eyes like waiting for some answer. Why are we doing this? Really there is this Kingdom an Ancient one with the thing called Magic and now there is a hope to revive it, so that it can perish again! Ajax continued his sentence. NO! We both can keep it alive, you see I am sure this kingdom is not evil, it never was, and we belong here we are the only ones maybe to be breathing. We may not let it die!!! "Yes" Ajax replied and with a "Got it" he told him that is something I need to tell you. Yeah go for it he told while brushing again(he had the brush in his hands all the time after brushing ones). I destroyed the the eternal sword. "What?", The Magical and the strongest sword in existence. Alberts eye popped and that's when Ajax added "and I detached the Ancient text", but don't worry it didn't affected the Text. What! Are You Serious! Don't be mad I found something, wait I'll bring them. He showed them to him and he asked What are these! Ohh wait could it possibily be! He went inside and told him to 'Stay there I am still Mad at you'. He went and came in some time later bringing the stone with carvings on the back. The stone with carvings of "4 4 inside you find it" written on the back. 4 4 it can be referring to 4 things placed on the place where it belongs, where it should be. Ajax eyes got big as he got excited, It makes sense he told. But the question is where? Albert asked. Right on the stone block you are holding Ajax said quickly. He took the heavy stone and put it down, then placed the golden pieces on it and Nothing happened. Ajax was going despondent but Albert let him know "We have to arrange them in perfect order". Some fast calculation and he instructed "16 possibilities there are so try and wait". He did so, placed in an order remembered it and changed it again and again. It was the 8 time when something did happened. Light started to come from the stone base and the golden pieces. It started to glow bright and suddenly light got reduced to a fixed amount. The color was dark yellow, The light and the things happening caused thair grandfather to wake up and come to see what was going on. What are you both doing? he asked. The right time, he replied. Wait wait I know what it is, the thing you activated. Activated? they both repeated, I have to think to recall the name now, old man told. Waaait! Tell us what is going to happen fast Albert asked. Old man looked at him but it was too late. The thing lifted 2feet high(very fast) and it blasted. All of them were pushed behind by the force but the blast didn't affected the thing. They went ahead and saw the thing covered in Blue, Green, Red and Yellow Fire. "Yeaahss" I remembered it is "obridor", Yeah that is what it is called. The purpose of this thing? Tell us grandfather we need to know! Yeah it is important! I am so sorry, I I just remember that I have to remember what I forget! "Huh", Recall what you forgot try it. I can't it was very strong magic, a curse to block the thought in the mind. I can just recall it was related to opening something big! Ajax said to grands 'Try to' but Albert interrupted him and said let it go. The information our dear Grands have provided is a big clue, we need to find where it connects. Ajax started to stare on the floating stone and was not able to distract his mind. He stepped ahead and... He had a unbearable headache, he saw Maya-Suki coming back from a place hot and burning. It was a place with hot black rocks and a place magical and reserved. It was a big place yes with a throne black and dark, the only color other than black was green! He saw her sitting on the throne but something was missing! That is it just this much vision and it's all over, the stone falled down. She is back! A Dark place and very hot, a throne, She is back Maya Suki he told fast. His grandfather calmed him, and Albert was in thoughts starring Ajax. Some time later when Ajax was all fine Albert asked where could this place be. A volcano! Ajax said, come on we know we cannot stay alive in there. Maybe Ajax is right, we used to gaurd our village from lava with magic and there are writtings reffering to a mysterious place in or on the volcanic mountain old man said. Wait grandfather you understand the language everybody of this island speaks asked Ajax. "Huhhuh" I was waiting for you to ask. Albert was quite. Tell us what is written he asked while holding the golden pieces. "Center", "Deep" "and" "Hot" it reads. Tell me, grands, what happened that day? How did everything end?? How, They Died??? We never died! It was a Big mistake by The Queen and everybody they all turned into dust and somehow I survived! Albert went and bought Lareme, opened a page and read. "No

Dead Human can be revived!", Perhaps The people who comes back through Death "They Never Died". Albert said You saw the Queen coming back and in your Deep thoughts and. The people performing a traditional dance in The Deep Thought Ajax completed. Hence we can conclude "The village, your peers and The Queen will be rejuvenated". Ajax then got an idea much more like a thought or a theory. He said, This could hurt you a bit old man, I have read in Lareme a Magic an automatic undo type of magic. That may unbind there curse, as we don't have any idea of what happened on (old man looked disappointed) that day. But there is just one thing, a problem. This can turn anybody evil and enlight their Demonic spirit!!! Albert with big eyes told that can be the reason. They have - turned - to the darker side of themselves. Noo! this can't be their grandfather reacted, unless we have a better explanation I am sticking with this belief, Albert announced. Brother I think I know something. "Umm", In the visions I just have, I saw Maya Suki without her Stick. Sticks that we carry are very powerful and holds much of the power of their user. It is a very strong weapon and a part of the soul, Old man said. Yeah and as their is stick mentioned in that riddle and Maya Suki being the strongest ruler and not have her stick as I saw her, we should find that stick. You sure you didn't saw it anywhere not even in the background Albert asked, "Sure" he replied. Then not bad bro, We shall do it... Our Old man moved ahead touched them both and teleported to a place, a room in particular. "Woohwooh", how many places like these you have Albert asked, Many many more he replied. It was a small room with a stone block and one thing on it. The Stick! Ajax screamed, Yeah I have this saved here for years. Wow, you have done quite a lot of work here Albert said. Thanks grandfather you saved us a lot of time he appreciated. Lets go we have it now he said. Noo we should keep the stick here for now, we can take it whenever we like Ajax suggested. Grandfather then teleported without wasting a second. 'Huh' these all things can surely worn-out a person like me. Grands I have got something to tell you Albert told and went to a distance for some walk and talk with his grandfather. Ajax was sitting inside in his shelter, he closed his eyes and started to remember all the things happened and the things only he saw. He started to feel hysterical, he was the only one who have little but seen the Danger lying ahead. There a little friend of him came by to check in. A nosorog who looked like an infant, Ajax spent some time with him and then released him. They both came back and Albert was enliven and came to remember "Milk!". You know brother your friendship with these hippo mouth can help us. How! he asked, Don't you know, you read the book alot I thought grands said. Read in the Milk section you will know how precious is there milk and difficult to obtain. He opened the book and:- Nosorog one of the hardest one when it comes to procuring their milk. It is known that their milk is one of the strongest produced by any creature or animal. Traces of Magic is found in their milk and contains high amount of energy in it. It is also used for brewing, mostly to enhance the effect of the potion. It is beleived to be a universal product. Got it! Albert asked after he finished reading, and Old man gave his hand for him to stand. Yeah "Thank You", So what are we waiting for lets go. Ok but remember they are very strong especially when in group Albert informed. Ajax now stood near their crash and moved ahead to pet one. They still beleived him. Old man came ahead and pet some of them too, he also invited Albert. Albert was confound of what he saw and moved ahead, his grandfather helped him pet one of them. All our humans were being familiar to animals of this little planet. They first played with them a lot and then in between kept Collecting milk as it was hard, everybody was running. It was Night now and they have 6litres of Nosorog milk!!! They went to Ajaxs made shelter, sat down, did some boiling and enjoyed the heavenly taste of Milk, They drank the lot of them. Everybody enjoyed a good night forgetting the danger and tension that lies ahead. Yeah and they slept on the grass below after enjoying the amazeball view of the sublime Night. "Wake upp!" A new day arrives, Ajax waked both of them at 8:00AM. They both waked up lazily and yawned, some minutes and they were ready for the day. Todays task to collect many flowers, weeds, wild plants, medicinal plants, seeds and a fruit. The intresting thing 90% of the things they need were magical They wore their needed clothes and Ajax and Albert were excited to see the things they never saw before. They walked to near the back of the island, there thought they can find some of them in the way. Well they did find one but the real thing were in front of them. They were standing in front of a 100,000 small plants with flowers and everything they needed. They collected everything they needed and maybe there wern't everything they needed. It took them 4hours to find everything except The Fruit. It took them another 2hours to find that fruit, they collected 6 of them. 3:33PM it was when they reached back to the shelter. There were many things but the mainly blue color fruit "Zegbeg" was the most important after the milk. They rested a bit and started to walk on the path to complete the brewing successfully. Step 1: To crush everything they had except the seeds, fruit and of course milk. Step 2: To add 6 drops of the milk and one big drop of honey in each of the crushed items. Step 3: To mix the specified item with each other and mix them properly(It would be good to mix them again). Step 4: Get a big cauldron and fill it with "Brenche"(a special type of date only found here), milk and holy water all in equal quantity. Step 5: Add a cup of everything made by flowers, weeds, wild plants, medicinal plants and 6seeds of everything mentioned in the cauldron. Step 6: Mix them with a stick of timber wood until it melts. Step 7: Finally add 1 Zegbeg in it and mix it again. Note: You have to wait for 16hours after completing the steps above, don't forget to mix it every 2minutes. The cauldron should be heated all the time on 1000degree C. After everything is done let it cool and filter it, only collect one glass of it the liquid left on the filter. The other should be boiled till everything is gone in air. They read it mainly Albert and he instructed them both to go and find the items and bring them when he reads and study more about it. They without any question or second thoughts were on it. Ajax brings the honey as he knew where it is and woods. Old man brings the Holy water and the cauldron and ect, Remember Maya Suki putting her head in it(the Holy water) as he knew it... Albert in the mean time crushing the items. It took them both 2 and 3hours to come back. Albert was done early and decided to make something cool and luscious at the same time. Some Collecting, cutting adding and flavouring and it was ready, it looked great too. They were there first grands then Ajax, They were happy and kind-of carefree. They have a bite and were so delightful to have it, It refreshed them and made them more energetic for the work ahead. So the pleasure ends and work comes. First fire, then ingredients, then water, milk and honey, then mixing, then the fruit, then boiling hot, then mixing-mixing-mixing and waiting the most important step. A hard task but they enjoyed. They sang songs, played some timepass games, saw the view of nature, remembered what they have been through and sleeping chance-by-chance. It was morning 9:00AM and it was warm from hot, it was time from filtration. They followed the step and had the dense liquid, they made it thin like water and 'wallah' they had it the Potion. Wait what is the name of the potion??? There is no name? Nope! There is this "AAA" written here. Ohh! Now I doubt it is the correct potion we made! Yeah it is I assure you. Okay here we go we have to turn these to vapours now so come on. They have the potion which they stored in a safe place. They took a rest for the rest of the day and gained some information about the island and it's history.

CHAPTER FIVE

Resurection Inside the Volcano

Here another new day, it has been more than a week now after coming to this island. Ajax was the first one to wake up and do some light training. It was not until little more than 10:00AM when everybody was truely awake. So now what to do? Old man asked. The stick, we should inspect it! Ajax told, and Albert nodded to it. Ajax and his grandfather went to bring it. While they were in that room before picking the stick grandfather said. I was the strongest one in the village! After The Queen! You wanted to be "The Strongest" Right! Who don't he replied and said I was trained by the Queen herself and would always be loyal to her. After that they teleported back with the stick held by Ajax. So what do we know Albert asked, Stick is a really powerful and an important thing Ajax replied. So what should we do then? Albert asked. To bring it's power outside to use it! he replied. "Yeeaahh" so how exactly we can do it? Albert asked. That's what he have to find... Ajax replied. What if I tell you I have! Albert said. Really you did? It was original your idea dumb oaf! What Ajax asked. To throw the stick inside the Volcano! Albert said with a crazy big smile. Whaaaat! That didn't worked, you know. Wait what did you threw in the volcano Ajax old man asked? Nothing some experiment... The sword you gave to him grandfather! What? why? why did you do that. Ajax was terrified. No need to scold him grands cause his idea was absolutely crazy and right. The lava in their happens to be a little different. It seems like what you call magic, can be explained by science Albert exclaimed. Well but their are still many things out of my reach so we should ignore it and move ahead he said. Then Albert took his bag and headed to the top of the volcano, he was walking when he told won't you both wanna to come! They had a nice walk but Grandfather had his own thoughts, he was quite and looking disappointed. They were there standing on the edge of the pit. They both saw everybodies face and Ajax moved to throw the stick. When he stopped and asked what happened to the sword? Albert replied it got cleaned and is safe now! believe me. Ajax was convinced and was just about to throw it, while Albert and Old man looked sharply. He threw it and in microseconds their grandfather jumped behind it. Albert said "Huh, Old man" and kicked Ajax quickly. Then he turned around and loosen his body to fall inside the volcano just like them both. It was a sight to be hold and even great if seen in slow motion, Everybody was falling to death Ajax thought. Their grandfather catched the Stick and threw it up, he was able to throw it in a way that missed both their bodies. They all were falling and Albert was right and grands too a little. A hole opened and they were just beneath the lava in a place big and dark. It is it? We are alive? Why did you? Ajax asked. Hey! I guessed this would happen and was glad you did too grandfather! That was when the stick came down and they saw something cool. They saw it reacting to the lava and it continued to react for some time even after landing. There they saw light moving around the stick covered in lava. Some seconds and Ajax saw the thing he wished to be here. "His Sword" it was deep in the rocks with its grip out. He hold that and bring it out! Strenght brother Albert said. Don't know you guessed it or not, there lack of knowledge are gonna get them, now! The lightening striked right on the Stick and created a force that pushed them far behind. They were pushed so behind that Ajax reached the Throne without walking and without his sword. There were lightening falling on the stick and many more, it was too strong to feel and resist. Ajax dropped some of the "AAA" liquid from the old bottle on the throne without knowing. The throne was so hot that the liquid started to evaporate but it got absorbed before evaporating. It was really hot there and everybody came together. Something from Alberts bag started to move, it was gaining speed and energy. He opened the bag and the Glass ball with the model of the island in it. It went in full speed towards the throne and crashed with it spilling the liquid inside. It gets even tense! Everybody was nervous especially Ajax. It was coming true "The visions". It was time, everybody suddenly stopped hearing anything and was just about to faint but they fold them and was awake feeling everything. They felt a vibration behind and turned back it was a red lightening type thing or some "chi". It was coming towards them and they covered their face as it passed through. They opened their eyes pointing the throne and they saw it.

ΔΔΔ

Her face it was Maya Suki Alive and stronger than before. She like a Queen walked to the throne and sat on it, just like Ajax saw. Old man walked ahead and came to a distance near her. She recognized him and said "Athanasios!". Albert said 'Your name' and Ajax continued 'She remembers'. Athanasios bowed down on his knee showing he is still loyal to her. "Don't" she said and continued "I'm sorry! for everything!" "You know what is going to happen" she said blankly. She looked traumatised and everybody was confused and ready. Her head suddenly bend down like if fainted while sitting. It was a minute of silence and she raised her head with a complete different attitude. She opened her red eyes and gave a dangerous look. She moved her hands straight ahead and her stick came towards her. Centuries it has been she said slowly and quitly to her stick. She banged her stick to the floor and stood up, and asked "What do you plan"! What does that mean Albert asked in his stance. You don't know! A fight awaits! and what are your plans for it she said. What are you telling! Ajax said. Be prepare! there is going to be a war! A unfair war, you 3 vs 20,000 troops, Including creature you can't imagine. What about you? Ajax asked! Don't count me I am not in this and if would be You would be glad, she replied in a suspicious way. And why worried you have got Athanasios on your side, I havn't seen anybody as strong as him. You can count on these two more, they are my grandson after all! Listening this and seeing their face with her emotional eyes, her brain was really working now. You! she told looking at Albert "Have my fathers Axe!". It would be a pleasure to give it back to you he replied. No! Keep it and use it as a weapon it will tell you everything you would ever know about it. She looked at our Old man and said use your weapons and brain you have a chance! Then she came to Ajax and gave him her stick and said In chess you should use your Queen instead of saving it or keeping it protected. This will help you and protect you, you should do the same! She looked at them all and said "Without memories you can't use your brain in a manner, So keep it safe!" Then She looked up and was gone(she teleported) in seconds with a blast of lightening. What should we do? Ajax asked but their grandfather teleported with them to the shelter taking the sword belonging to Ajax. The Sky was dark and their was a Thunderstorm it is going to be something big and something never seen before. Where should we go now! Albert asked, You will know! he replied. Listen there is going to be a combat ahead and Ajax cut off his sentence and said This is no combat we 3 vs 20,000 dangerous things coming to kill us. Yeah! Maybe they are on the way coming to kill us now Albert added. Then you will see my Power never have you seen before, just wait sons you are going to be paralyzed after seeing it! "How do he get these sentence" Albert said to Ajax and he replied "It dosn't makes sense". Pay attention you both cause it looks like it is going to rise Athanasios said while looking at the ocean. So wha, They all teleported to a place not to familiar, Stop cutting my sentence Ajax said. What is going to happen said Albert, The sky it's turning Red said Albert, So it looks like it is going to happen huh said Athanasios. Alright tell us everything first, no suspense Ajax asked his grandfather. This sky, Rain, Lightening, and everything I am seeing, this reminds me. It is going to rise, a big layer of solid land spreading as far as kms away. The water it is going to go back like in low tides he said. But in thunderstorms isn't the land should be covered in water? Albert asked. Don't forget this is a magical island brother Ajax said and with some excitement his grandfather said Yes you guessed it. A problem that islands face, drowning in the ocean but we removed a solution for it too. Ok ok, so now what are we supposed to do? Albert asked. With a deep long breathe, making them both nervous their grandfather said "Wait!". They got the most releaf but they wih the help of their grandfather went and brought many things before sitting down on the wet rocks and the rain disabling their pleasure to sleep. They had many things in a water proof bag and were ready to fight. It was not until half an hour that "It started to happen". "The Strong wind, hurting rain and the fear to die." Soon they could see something coming for them. They were ready. Athanasios with his unique stick, Ajax with the stick that the Queen gave him and Albert with the heavy powerful Axe. Standing like heros their fear started to end. "Kaboom" lightening striked and they saw a flash of them which looked like 20,000 flying thing coming towards them. Thoes looked like flying dinosaurs and were about 6 to 8feet in height. "Yeaah! It's going to be exhilarating!", Old man said. "Yeah! this is crazy and making me feel intoxicated!", Ajax said. Stop using words, don't you understand these would be some freaking strong creatures which can fly and they are 19,997 more than us in number! Albert said to them. Why is this man here ~Ajax, He doesn't understand ~grandfather. Stop doing that and use what you've got Albert said, I expect that from you too son his grandfather told. Those flying things came close and something strange happened. They saw the 20,000+ flying creature shrink in size and turn into a 2cm small in height. They looked much of Dragonfly and Butterfly combined. There were constantly attacking which went on for some time until. Use your brain you too and see this. He moved the stick up and a lightening striked on it and him controlling it released it in air. Which caused everybody to get shocked, this is what you call using of brain Albert commented. But anyways it borrowed them some time to come with a plan as the flying things were down. Their plan was a chaos of their own ideas. Their ideas was crazy and it was like they were not in consciousness. Their ideas were like burning them as soon as possible, catching them all, And Eating them, these ideas are disgusting. The small creatures were up and their plague were ready to do what they were really good at "Kill". Our heros with no plan and a lot of irritation and frustration because there were thousands of insects bigger than mosquito all around them. The crazy thing they were not physically affected by the harsh rain. The three of them were just killing the things in the air and it was just 31minutes and every one of them were gone. Everyone, all 20,000 flying insect were dead down. Ajax, Albert and Athanasios were losing their mind, they sat down and were not able to think rationally. Ajax came near them both and hold their hands seeing his grandfather and they teleported. After teleporting our old man was seeing Ajax with a hesitating face. "Thank you!", Albert said to both of them and asked what was happening. Don't know Ajax replied. Rest! you both, we won, their grandfather said, and they just lay down slowly gaining their consciousness. It was day, they were so weak they couldn't hold to do anything but to sleep on their bed the past night. Ajax and Albert woke and came up, they were not so surprised to see our Old Man looking at the sun up in the sky. Now? Ajax asked his grandfather and he replied 'a bit later'. See the sky it is shining today grandfather told, Remember the word, "Shining" he bolded. I will! Ajax replied, ok Albert said to his sentence. So now tell us, sorry to interrupt but can you remember this number forever too old man said after interrupting Albert. "Yeah" Ajax said, "Say it" Albert replied. 4,784,484 remember this forever he said, will try he replied. So tell me now, grandfather, what do you think! Albert asked while fidgeting with the model of the island with brocken glass. Circumstances tells and I know some more than you do, for now he replied. It showes the Deep Thought and the visions later and what she did and her incredible skills she is exceptionally different. We can believe that she has been cursed and she hasn't overcome it yet but I would suggest to investigate some more, Ajax said. It is hard to believe grandfather said on his words. Some seconds later Albert asked to old man "Something I wanted to ask again, Who is your mother, our great grandmother?" I don't know he replied. Should we go finding her? grandfather asked them both. Noo! replied Albert and said we have to prepare! Then Ajax came in their conversation and said "Every help we could find every weapon and the power we possess, our strenght!". I don't know what but something bad is going to happen and we have to be ready for it. Okay Albert replied with some surprise and asked 'What to do next then?' That's your work brother he replied. Albert with the weird face said I knew that. Then turned to his grandfather and asked "Tell me everything you know about her". There is a lot! You can never know everything! but I may tell everything important things about her. First thing first, she was never bad and cared about everybody. The strongest queen in the history, has a ton of secrets. More! Ajax asked. Yeah! learn to have patience Ajax! he replied. Sorry! he committed. Then she is highly manipulating and her style is to trap the person in his own talks, you understand right he asked and they nodded their head. He continued, she can be extra dangerous and can take things to extream levels. The important thing, She has the potential to break the limits! And I may commit she is the strongest Magic user alive now, he told slowly with his head down. Our Queen back in the days was the strongest and I the second, she was really kind and was a family to me, "I never knew who was my mother!" There are many things but these are the most important ones. Grands you are the best amongst us Albert said and then they all started to come with a idea, to predict the next move of Maya Suki. It was time when Albert stood up and said what Ajax told before. "We shall believe what Ajax saw and work according to him and his visions" he said. The women from the throne which is Maya Suki, that means she is going to lead an attack with many creatures. And I too saw the people dancing their dance what can that mean Ajax told and asked. People are going to step on this island some how Albert said, Maybe like the Queen grandfather suggested. These talks why they have to be so dense their grandfather said, this sentence attracted their boths attention. "What" he asked, "Nothing" they both replied. "Think", we will have a talk in a while said Albert and left for a walk followed by Ajax. Everybody was on their own quite and deep in thoughts. It was sure enough something big is going to happen. It was a half an hour or so they meet again in silence, Ajax maked his move. He told "The stone", that purple memory stone I need it, can you Ajax asked to his grandfather. I umm he wasn't able to decide. Don't worry I understand its importance and just want it to have a closer look! he said. You know it is very powerful and dangerous, it's a thing I don't know much about. I know believe me I will take care he said. Well, I trust you but be careful you really have too. You would have guessed it brother, "It can destroy your mind" Albert warned Ajax Okay he replied. Don't get infected Albert said. Well grandfather, I need to ask! I am going to have some inspection of this island, a research of some kind he said. And as the area of this Island is so big it can take some time. So, You can, no worries Old man allowed, how much time maximum will you take he asked. A week he replied. Great! I was thinking of translating the Ancient Text too grandfather said. Soo it looks like we are going to be on our own Ajax said. Yeah! grandfather said, Albert was quite and then said. The next time we meet it will be fantabulous!!! It is it 5minutes later everybody was ready to go. They gave a charming smile and were on their way. Ajax with the purple stone had his own plans. Albert was in a doubt and filled with crazy theories and ideas. Where Athanasios was stressing his brain, trying to remember the things he has forgotten. Ajax quickly took some gunpowder(300g) and with a lighter, a piece of paper and a big rope ran towards the well in the ruins of the village. There without any second thought he jumped in the well. He didn't got hurt as he tied the rope to a strong place and he held it strong too. There he threw all the gunpowder he had went a distance away burnt the paper and threw it. The gunpowder burned but didn't blasted strong. He just wanted to see if their was any other place other than what he breaked before. He found nothing and went back, it took an hour and half to do it all. But he cleared his doubt. He sat down in his shelter and was thinking about what he would have missed? and what to do next? Some minutes and he was up with a new idea. He made some fire and placed his sword on it to enhance its power. Then he quickly with the purple crystal went to the peak of the volcano. There he wanted some lava so he used a tungsten made bucket, attached to a big fat rope. (He bought it with him) Slowly he released the rope, filled in some lava, and lifted it back up. He has it now, without damaging the rope. He again went back to his place and knew what to do. He had listen from his grandfather and read in the collected notes and book his grandfather had on this island, which they both were reading. He knew "Every Strong Magical Object and Entity will show it's Power if Engaged or Attacked by a Strong or Powerful Force of Energy or an Object." So first just one drop of the potion they made he poured on top of it. Followed by some hot Lava, it took some time so he waited. Nothing happened! He had a feeling it wont so he had his sword. He took it up and smashed it on the crystal, nothing much happened just some sparks came out. He smashed it again and again, each time the sparks and its inner heat increased. He had enough and like a "Controller of the Sword" he with the power of his spiritful energy stored his power. Then striked it on the stone, The stone didn't cracked. But it started to glow hard with some spark coming out of it time-to-time. He gave a last powerful strike and then threw the stone in the lave bucket. He forgot about it after that. Meanwhile, He went to meet different creatures, animals of this Island! He saw many of em and were able to tame some with his unique TACTICs. He saw a animal he described like an different type of Crocodiles. A "V" shaped snout, sharp and strapping teeths, A muscular heavy body, sharp glaring eyes and a funny tail. He wanted to go forward and have a closer look but they were to aggresive. They looked like a still body with moving eyes and Ajax felt something. He knew what it was and after some minutes he walked away. He saw another animal which was an horse in another form. He was probably till now thinking these all were like a childs play but there was some thoughts of his enough to proof it wrong. First, It all was real and really happening. Second, There was a reasonable, deep and consequent reason behind it. Third, The island have a long, different, harsh and a bit sad history, regarding to its origin. He found them interesting, big and calm at that time so he moved ahead to make his move. He wanted to win their trust and wanted to ride them once as his own wish. Well, first two things were right but don't know about 'calm'. Cause when he came ahead to touch his head it kick him hard and the next moment he was their 4feet away holding his back. He stood up and tried again. This time he removed his sword and things. He removed some cherries he bought as he knew this would happen. He offered it to them but they were angry and protecting themselves by trying to stand up. He backed off several times until he removed a sound like them "Uaarrrrrrhh". They were stunned, it was a thing to, be adapted to it so fast. Here some more sounds and food and they were already his friends. He made 1 more animal friend and got shued away many many times. He was back from where he started and was happy to see grandfather sitting their. After reaching, he told "A Good Day it was." Yeah sure, a bit busy for me he replied. Well what did you do he asked. "Yeeaah" you should know this I am looking for the book where everything about our language is written down, and I think I am close. That's great Old man he said with minimum satisfaction. Your Old Man just happens to be the strongest from all and the best too, I hope he said. Don't worry grandfather you are, being kind with us and not acting as great you should, you really are Ajax said. Then with a smile they had some thought like the need of having a bonding with the animals for help and things like this. Then Ajax was outside seeing the sky, sleeping in his shelter and grandfather in his comfy room, after eating the food made by our old man. Ajax opened his eyes and it was almost 1PM. A big yawn and he started the day lazy, winding up the minor things he started making his lunch. A matter of time he said after eating his lunch and back to work. Now a big rock he took and breaked the lava which was hard now, he did it till the purple thing was free. He cleaned it well and hold it firmly, and something happened. It started to show visions of the past. It changed uncontrollably 'the visions', all about time until it showed Ajax and Albert fixing their projector at their home. Then, 'Damb' the stone fell from his hands and it stopped. He picked it up again and thought about him sitting on a throne with his own stick. His grip got even tight and it showed what he wanted it to "Him sitting on a throne with a stick". He soon knew it was not just what it looks and much more prominent and significant. The minute he knew about it he rushed to grandfather to take him(teleport him) to his place where they gained information about the island and rested. This because Albert had Lareme and the book that had knowledge abut this purple stone was there, in a book he saw before. They where their and Athanasios left Ajax their for his peace. He read everything and said "Yeah I knew saving it for now would be a good thing and I knew the basics thanks to these books". He kept reading, after finishing one, he found more related to it, "He loves reading", he too checked the one he had read before to highlight the important things. It was already 9PM and he had read many books related to the island and the stuff inside it(the island). He came up from the stairs and reached his place till 9:34PM or little more. He was content to see his grandfather with fresh and delectable food ready to be served. He reached their and gave a smile, come on dinner is ready old man said. Thanks he thanked and both enjoyed a great dinner, old man told Ajax that. I am going to a place on an island for 2days so look for yourself. Sure he replied, the meal was very good he said and went to sleep, today on a bed. Ajax was asleep after a quite day, were Albert hunted for something strange and unusual. Not to forget inspecting the big areas of the island filled with danger. A big yawn and Ajax was up, it was 11:00AM and he said "I started to miss good night sleeps!" He got ready for the day and then tried a crazy thing, "To copy Thor!" He was trying to bring the sword to him like thors hammer. "Yeah" he failed and then he gave himself a suggestion, "To end the childish behaviour." Watching the sun thinking what would be the best thing to do. He decided to work on developing him as much as he can. This means to take his power, inner energy, strenght, weapon training and knowledge to a whole new level. He said, "Here we go", then realised and looked left and right, he said to himself "I am alone". So he took the stone in his hand and with a very heavy bag(60kg) walked to the shelter he made. He thought the heavy bag would increase his strenght and he can exercise with the purple crystle if to fulfill what he thought he has to do with it. He was trying to feel the wind, absorbing the energy of nature and built up his own magical abilities. It is said that amethyst(purple crystle) is way stranger and unknown that it is know. It has the faculty and propensity of absorbing any sort of magic it is deliberately(Stronger) or naturally(Weaker) when bought in contact with. He was walking for 6minutes now, in the hope he is charging the stone in his hand. Now, he kept his eyes open and imagined about a hundred people in a room listening to the live perform of his favourite singer(which didn't happened in real life). He adjure the amethyst to show what he imagined, and I didn't thought it would be so easy he said out loud. He could see what he imagined so easily, without using much of his energy, don't forget he is under pressure of that much weight he is carrying on his back. Well he could see his destination now, he was wondering about what all things can he do with magic or an average person or his grandfather. He was there and without wasting a second he started his training. Another day gone in training he said, it was 11PM now and he was to sleep while reading a book. A short night for him, he slept near 1AM and waked up at 4AM. After brushing his teeth he was up, he had a list of what all to do today. And believe me he did it all with or without any pain. First off 2hours of warm ups, a fascinating thing he could lift more than a 100kg. Then 3hours went in things like push-ups and running, he can run really fast Really, he did more things. Then the other 2 an a half hours went in meditation, it really helped him building his inner strenght. A break till 9AM in the strong sun rays. Up again with some rough weapons and practicing the art of sword fighting and fighting with different sticks and other weapons, this went on for 2hours. Now comes the worst stage of his training "Maximum suffering". He made the boiling waters of the hot spring even hotter and then sat in there for half an hour. Before that he hold his breathe underwater for 16min, 7min, and 28min that was a serious and risky suffering. He came out hot and burned but his determination was not yet brocken. The next instant crazy thing he did was tying himself with a weight of 50kg and hanging to the cliff. If he fell, he would find himself in the depth of deadly water currents. He successfully completed his goal of half an hour infact it was more than it. It was not over yet he continued these all for more time. In total it was 8hours of harsh, deadly and breathtaking activities he did after the warm up, weapon use, meditation and more. He was crazy tired but still willing to go on. It was late in night already and yeah he took 5minutes breaks in between. A fact he didn't ate any food all day, and now was determined not to sleep and he didn't! He was sitting straight and breathing calmly after all the things he have did. He was just thinking about energy flowing all around him or he was seeing! He was in this trance till 4 in the morning and yeah again he go, but before, He took a Bath, brushed his teeths and all the minor things like that. "Up ahead and Ready to go", He started what he was doing yesterday. He didn't care for himself and the hours passed on. It was nearly 5PM and he was out from the hot waters now from 1 an a half hour he has been. He was exhausted but had strenght to do no more. He was running which turned into walking towards the place he called home. He was almost there which was his task but something happened. He saw Albert and grandfather individual coming to the place he made, they didn't knew they both were heading to the same place. And then, The last glance and everything was black, "he fainted". They both rushed for him and was hoping it was not badder than it. They discovered him down again, he was breathing! His energy was over for the sake of energy itself they thought. They waited and helped him wake up every second He was sluggish and on the edge, he was feed food and he drank water, he sat taking support of the tree. What were you doing? Albert asked, Athanasios with his hands on his head was bombshelled and startled. The question is how are you alive he told and asked to Albert and Ajax! You are going to tell me everything you did after taking a proper rest old man said and left. Why now brother! We need you! Albert said and sat along side him. 40minutes later we see grandfather and Albert standing and talking. Ajax was down still sitting, not for long! He came in proper consciousness and took a stand, they turned. "Yeah" Albert said and smiled after seeing him and Athanasios, happy from inside and equally curious, he changed his attitude. They all have another thing in common now "Their Serious and Strong Attitude". Brother, Something else might be going on ~Albert. The words of Royalty, screaming over ~Athanasios. We have to be ready it can happen anytime Old man said. The greater power might be our enemy and if not, "We are fighting a Blind War!" Albert said.

CHAPTER SIX

The Collaboration to Fight the Truth

They were standing without a moment, all serious and patient, waiting for the thing to come out when, something unexpected happened. Athanasios hands touched them on shoulder and they are gone, all of them teleported to the place you know. The place were they talked to their grandfather for the first time. The Throne, Black hot rocks and The Lava. They reached their and the next second everything changed. They all were down on the ground, invisible and light. They saw the things impossible to tell fake, it was happening right in front of them. They saw Athanasios first, Standing in front of the text and arranging it like it was before. He seemed sad and again lost in thoughts. It switched to Ajax laying down and reading the book until his head goes down and he is deep in sleep. It changed to Albert sitting down, taking support of a brocken house in the Ruins. His head was down and was he worried. Next about Ajax doing the things he did for the stone to show his power. It was changing rapidly and they were seeing everything in pain. It came to Athanasios who was standing with his glowing hands on a text trying something to read it. Albert now, he was walking around the ruins and breaking the brocken houses, ect in the name of finding something. It switched to another of his clip where he was throwing stones to a place we are familiar with. Then it switched to grandfather digging a place, he was already deep enough where he found a floor of brick. Ajax now walking with amethyst making hallucination. Then to their grandfather again. It was morning and he was training hard and much more sensible than Ajax. It then switched to Albert who was somewhere not so common, There were many plants moving their face in different direction catching birds. They were big in size and Albert was standing in front of them with The Axe. It again changed to Ajax now just hanging to a cliff with rocks tied to him. Then our old man who was meeting a medium sized creature who suddenly became double of its size when he was trying to touch him. The thing was like a puffer fish but he "puff up" way more than a puffer fish can ever do, he had spines almost all over his body. The purple crystle showed many things, reveling what they did when they were off finding things to help the situation which was also the cause of them separating. It was a long way until it ended, they were already in pain, the reason. When Athanasios teleported with them both, Ajax was holding the stone tight, it made a chain with them all connected by hands. It takes a hell lot of energy to teleport, not till you master it. The energy reacted with the amethyst passing a strong current through their bodies. The current was strong enough to let them down and take the things they were recently thinking and show it in the form of its magic. They were up and Ajax asked who? when? Albert added while seeing down, We need cooperation don't you get it. I have things to show, and the stone it tells it grandfather said. We all do! Ajax replied and then said not this way. Sorry now, but listen to me old man pleased. I got it the answers to the text! he said. I have many things you would want to know too Albert said. Well, I have a thing which may fascinate you, this was Ajax. I have taken care for the missing things Albert responded. But why here! he asked to grandfather. Cause I found this, A thing which was hidden by one of the People Of Vasílissa, I kept it here. What is it? Ajax asked. Listen I found this, I remember, It is this potion, A potion of Magic, I would say. The potion enhancing your skills, your magic!(he told with his fingers on Ajaxs chest) This allowing us to make unbelievable things from our hands, a potion Dangerous even. Only 5 were made, or were possible. It had a deep history and a thing, A prophecy, not to important I said before but now I think. It said all to be consumed together but it dosn't says what will happen if not, Grandfather said. Your turn he passed to Albert. Well, no speech going on, no one here to listen. But I found these 3 things with the myth you were carrying Ajax. I have these 6 green diamond shape things, strong like hell. I figured this out, it could not get out of reach from each other. I threw it away but they attracted it after crossing a distance. It had something, remember The stones that fitted, far from further away, he said. You know there was one plate I guess inside the soil of the moving plants. So I dig it up and there are two thing I found. Then here I was walking on the beach small one, finding something I believed to be. And here I find this, no idea how but I find this on the sand not deep and brocken. I found the other part of it in someones house, the story you told us, grandfather!

"Peoples Houses". It seems it was more than a story, it's a charm. Yeah you all didn't have cameras back in your times, but your power of love, magic and friendship made this immortal according to me. Your friends still helped you, now, it has the capability of ending the curse or part of it. here, you have your forgotten memories back, Albert said. Huh, you did! his grandfather reacted reacted. Well, it is my honor to have it but just a little later, I will use. Thank you, Really and let Ajax say now he said. Yeah, So listen I found the ultimate way to make yourself stronger, in many ways. But this is the thing to be amazed of he said and asked his grandfather to teleport everyone on the grounds, this time the energy didn't overflowed and no current was past. There, holding the amethyst, seeing in their eyes, he used all his power to project an "Army". It was all there an army of 500 or more armoured people with weapons and their stances. It was dark and impossible to detect it was false, He even projected himself by being a leader of em. He also have the capability to cast a hot, dark and volcanic effect, like a climate is. How can you imagine so deep! Albert asked. That's what I did from when I was a child Ajax replied. He ended the illusion stunning them both, especially Athanasios. The picture, the illusion was mind blowing and impossible to tell it was fake, it drained much of Ajaxs energy thou. There they stand again, Bold and confound. Ajax then said So it's all over when his grandfather replied just one last thing. I have this cube one made in our time by I don't know who. Ajax took the cube for closer inspection while old man continues. It was believed to be made by an unknow person from our village. The cube is strong and hides many secrets from our time, it is also know to have many many charms, hex, curses and spell performed on it. No one in our time was able to solve it, No one, And I found it in a room we made long-long time ago. I was shocked seeing this thing sitting there, from how much time I don't know. It seems like he(the creator of the cude) was on to something at that time. And here Ajax have it, The cube he solved it like nothing. Just an ordinary 3 by 3 cube it looks to me, he said. Well you have no idea, what might you have done Old man told in shock, You sure it is real Albert asked. Yess I am sure he replied. Then it's just a matter of time, while I, we have things to tell you Albert said to Ajax. It is, we saw big armies of all sorts of creature and people alike, they looked similar from the dancing men you described Albert said. I saw the queen looking ready like before, ready for a fight, It can happen anytime grandfather added. She is here on the island, she is preparing for something, which can harm us. So it's about us, we have to decide what we have to do and we have to do it fast Albert told. I know what to do! Ajax announced. We have no idea where she is or what she is doing so we have to be ready right. Guess what if you say there is a war ahead, "We will fight", using our brain. We shall rest on guard till it is time today, and it will be the night. I will go to a place, it is important and you both we go for the volcano top. If the information you both have provided me is right, something is going to happen, and night is the time. We have to use every weapon, every power we have, We all are really strong so just show it. He took a long breath and continued, if she attacks us with her army we have ours. What Albert asked, I can make an army and we have our animal friends he replied. Mainly it's about our power and potential, we have to use it for a future to exist on this island, this sentence opened their eyes. We don't know the situation yet so when we do we will take action accordingly he said. Like a true politician Albert whispered to his grandfather, and they shared a laugh. Well we can unlock the mysteries unsolved instead of resting if you like he asked. The things you told were just like a leaders word and yeah we shall Albert replied. I know what does the Text say, I can tell Athanasios said. It is mostly about biographies of the Four Rulers but it have hidden messages. There are many in many ways and it will take time to understand. Old man just finished his sentence when this happened. Diamonds in the front, just sitting without a moment, it appeared out of nowhere. Then something more happened, A great pain in the minds of all. It wasn't a headache cause it was hurting bad. The pain lasted for about a 30 seconds and something, a memory, was what they can see. They never were there but they can see it now, inside their head. It was about a tree located not far from shore, it was like a mango tree but was different in many ways. Then they could suddenly see the interior were there was a box hiding something inside. They rushed to the location after seeing this and reaching there Albert cut the portion of the tree and found it. The box, just like they saw, It was not big and there was a place on top of it for a hexagon diamond it looked like. The one that we saw before Ajax asked and Albert replied No I know what we need, then he rushed to his bag and removed the diamond that was needed. How do you have it? Ajax asked, well it didn't worked on it Albert said, What? he asked again, You will know he replied. And it opened, they saw a piece of paper, it read "The enemy of enemy, The creator, The Ruler I become, A kind heart locked in greed, I possess the power no one feeds." They all looked each other and then we see them back standing in front of the shelter. What does it mean! Albert asked, It dosn't matters his time is over and I hope it wont affect us grandfather told. They all waited for some time and then were off to see what happens with the new plate and six diamonds Albert found. Lets see what happens grandfather said seeing those things, Well, your finds made ours low Albert said to him. Lets see he placed them all and a strong force was made from doing so. So what happened! Ajax asked Albert went to a distance and threw a stone at him. It bounced back! Yeah, I knew Albert shouted. Grandfather told a shield it makes, now I remember when hiding the treasure. It can be very useful Ajax said. There are so many things more to know, to discover, There are just so many mysteries we know about but just not the solution and the Truth about them Ajax said. I promise you will, we will I may say, I promise we will know everything together. All the great things left behind, to know more about the things we have been through but after his situation created is over. We will know more after we know what is going on here and solve this, we will explore the Universe of Nekrós Lieweg together I promise his grandfather replied. I'll be waiting Albert said, that's what I want you too old man replied. Okay now just some work and then some rest and there it is the Big night Old man said. They prepared by bringing everything every power together, all the weapons. Then like a 2 hours later they were just sitting with their legs fold, just feeling the wind. They spend an hour of theirs doing nothing but sitting and feeling the winds. They knew this is going to help them a lot. They had a craving for food and so they ate a delicious plate of it and then just rested. They were thinking, trying to figure out what can be real, better plans and stuff like that. It was little more than 9PM when they started to be ready. After eating some food and warming up, they had a look around the island watching for spies, they thought. Nothing happened it was all quite and silence, they could only hear the sounds of nature. It was so tranquil, that it somewhere inside made them fearful of what stands ahead. They knew it was a game of death and they could die anytime but they were still up for a reason good enough. It was like this till midnight, they were up as our old man told them what time was it, he was quite used to it. Then it happens.

ΔΔΔ

Here we stand to an end, don't forget this Ajax said. Ajax leaves with a big bagpack with everything he needs, he choosed the long path to the ruins, which took him an hour to reach. Our other heros were for the peak and they reached their earlier than him. There he stands, ready to climb the top of the Great Tower, now brocken. But then he saw something, someone was spying, he saw the figure in the dark and there he runs. Ajax chased him, he was fast but our hero isn't less. He was so close to catch him when he disappeared. On the other hand Albert and Athanasios saw fire on the other side of the island and ran to check what was it. It has been half an hour as Ajax tries to catch the dark thing disappearing and appearing again and again, and they both finds the cause of fire, It was 1:45AM. The thing was in front of Ajax, when he transformed into a ball of light and went up in the sky attracting Alberts attention. They both run for the spot the light was conjured, Ajax was going for the great tower again in disappointment. They both were worried and decided to take the potion Athanasios found(the 5 bottles of the potion). They drank the potion so that they can increase their speed to help Ajax, who they thought would need help. They knew it would do way more than just increasing their speed. Ajax was standing on top of the tower from 3minutes. So he took a seat, they were too far from him but the potion made it possible for them to reach for him fast. They looked each other and that's when old man realized today is the Blue moon day. Their body looked like it was their ghost, just like Ajax saw! Isn't it special for brothers Albert asked. Yeah but how do you know that? I heard it, a voice speaking "It is near", "The Blue Moon Day", I saw letters two, but of a language I didn't knew. It told more about it and I saw Ajax, It was the night I reached the island and when I woke up it was already night so. I took an piece of paper attached it to a arrow and launched it in the Sky as a sign of love and help for my brother. I don't know what happened to it and forgot about it in all the things that we were doing, Albert said. Yeah the potion reacts with the moonlight on this night and makes the consumers more powerful and light as a ghostly figure. Fast we got to go Albert realized. They were there and wanted him to drink it too as it says, everyone has to drink it together. Ajax saw them just like in the visions and was scared, they quickly told him to take the potion and so he did. It was a seconds pause and they were just standing seeing the sky, Ajax thought they were dead and flying. Then it happened again, the effect from the cube that was solved, it showed them all another of it(the vision for pain). It showed the cliff with no humans yet, from were they could see an army of animals, birds, fish and armed people. Beside they saw people dancing in a traditional way with fire around them, it too showed they can make a hole with the help of the potion they had. It ended without much pain and, they were speechless. They took a long breath still seeing at the sky, and Ajax was relaxed now. Then it happened, they both falled down and with the help of circular hole they made in air, they were their on the cliff and now there were humans infact two of them(Albert and Athanasios). Here Ajax fades in dark pink light but with a smile. He reached were they both already were and with a strong "Bang" on the ground with the stick Maya Suki gave him he made a strong force forcing them see behind. Where Ajax was sitting like a King but on a rock. "Yeah", this time grandfather said and their ghostly effect was gone. Well, Ajax was not looking ghostly like them, it takes some time for the effect to go naturally, The effect was gone because the moon was hidden by the dark clouds. They all were seeing her army and people performing their traditional dance. Old man told them both it can be a ceremony of the return of the Queen and The People Of Vasílissa, My friends. This is no time to be celebrating, they might be under control of the dark power, of the dark magic Albert said. Well there is a 100Tales nursery rhymes to make evil and demons pure. Be serious grandfather Albert reacted. The Queen and everybody were now starring at them and it was there time to be ready. Athanasios was ready with his stick in his one hand and the pendant Albert returned him in other, he had many other weapons all over his body. Albert was ready with the Axe and a ball of his energy in his hands(Any magic user can make one, as strong the person is the energy ball will be more powerful). Ajax with his Stick given by the Queen in one hand and the purple crystle in another. They were all armed with their armour and had many weapons. Ajax and Athanasios slammed their metal sticks on ground together and. Ajaxs stick got opened a little and a flute came out of it. He showed them and they were surprised, he tried to play it and Failed. Nothing happened but then he again tried with all the feelings he could gather and a beautiful sound came out. The pure sound made all the creature including humans calm down, it was like he was controlling them. It didn't seemed to affect Maya Suki though. But then he stopped and everyones(all creatures including humans) rage back. They completed their dance and now it looked like it was the time for them to attack. Albert was waiting for a moment to stun everybody and it happens now. Ajax used the amethyst and created an illusion of more than 10,000 armed soldier right in front of the queens army. It was Alberts moment to shine he removed a yellow crystal with a 100 sides and used its powers to bring the artificial life in the soldier Ajax made. The soldier were controlled by them now and were living on the energy the crystal provided, You know it now Albert said to Ajax with a strong and happy smile. "Yeeaah" Old man screamed and the Queen stepped ahead. He was coming to destroy their army, Ajax removed a loud noise and grandfather did the same thing but their noises were different. She was destroying their soldires when Ajax screamed ("Ahhhhh") and jumped high to attack the queen. His stick transformed into a sword from top and he was covered in reddish yellow energy making him look like covered in fire. He attacked the Queen with full power but she blocked it just with her hand. The Fight officially begins! Albert told his grandfather come on don't you wanna join and jumped to help his brother. Old man said I thought I would be but you both are the leader, Great! and made his jump. All three of em were fighting the Queen but she was alone taking all their attacks and was she not behind showing her power. Albert then saw the loyal soldier of the Queen coming for them and moved ahead to defend his family. Where Athanasios knew how strong can the people of Vasílissa can be so he went there to stop the people he is one among. Means Ajax was alone fighting the Queen, He was strong enough to last long. All sorts of curses, spells and use of energy was taking place, it looked like everybody wanted to kill each other. The fight was on for 15minutes now and nobody was about to quite. The fight was getting intense and She threw Ajax far away knocking him down. His stick was nowhere to be found but he could see the Magical sword of his which he dropped down a distance away. She was coming ahead with her stick, she transformed it to a very powerful sword and took her run. She jumped high with madness and a laugh, she was just about to use her sword on him when. Ajax believed in himself and attracted the sword towards his hand while standing up. She striked her sword on him and Ajax attacked with his sword right on hers. A force created, a force so strong that made everybody fall was created. Everybody was down except for them both, they were sword fighting now. The fight was getting really dangerous now, Maya Suki who is also known for her control over her emotions was in Rage and Ajax was no exception. Two powerful bodies of energy and crazy power, both in Rage were against each other. Albert and Athanasios knew if this continued they both would end up destroying the whole island in some time. But then something happened!

ΔΔΔ

Thunder clouds gathered, lightning started to strike very hard and everybody felt, something is going to happen. The fight was still on until, They saw up at the Sky and the thing everybody sees was extraordinary. Everybody saw as a lightning seems to come towards them like it is a meteoroid falling at full speed. It was way bigger and broader than any lightning ever would have striked, By its speed it looked like it was coming from space. Just like Ajax saw in his visions! Maya Suki was stunned and said "Noo", looked at Ajax and told him "I am not your enemy". She was worried, and she collected all energy she could in a second and took a powerful jump, she was flying faster than a rocket. Ajax hold her hands when she was about to take off Thus, he was up with her. She looked him with big eyes and he said "Now". The Queen understood that, and launched Ajax in a speed very very fast, faster than her. She launched him towards the thing leading the lightning. She followed Ajax and in full speed came there to help. Ajax crashed to the thing making his speed a little slow, It looked like double boom exploded strong in the sky from down! Ajaxs speed was exceptionally fast! Down on ground everybody stopped fighting and was looking up at the sky. Maya Suki crashed just a second later after Ajax making him even slow. They both up in the sky tried their best to stop it and down on ground Athanasios and Ajax launched in full speed in order to help. It took them 23 seconds to reach where the queen and Ajax were 19seconds more then them. They all used everything they had got and stopped the person leading the lightning from smashing on the island. They have saved it, "Nekrós Lieweg", from dying! But all four of em were hurt very badly from the lightening and the immense pressure they have to go through. For the first time they could see it a man made of metal, What is this? Albert asked. The Guard to be summoned when violations out of control, It was created by the Great Fours energy combined. And it returns means!!! What can we do? What is gonna happen? Ajax asked! We have to finish it which is not going to be easy, even for me! This is the first time she said. Be ready you three and direct your soldiers to fight for the Sake of the island and everybody she said loudly for everybody to know. She instructed her army to do the same, then she said "Now you shall see the Power of the Greatest Ruler that exists!" Your the boss Ajax ~Albert, Yeah lead us ~Athanasios. O-Ok he said and together with Maya Suki screamed for the army to attack the Enemy. Lithorous! this is the name of the artificial God made by the Rulers! His height is about 9.6feet, and possess the power of the 7elements. A Guardian made to protect the violation of the law of nature of the island. Impossible to be destroyed, you don't stand a chance to defeat his mighty protector. Everybody the Nosorogs, Sthenarós, the puffer fish animal, evry animal Ajax, Albert and Athanasios meet and many more, like türemgii and Turba they all now had a common enemy the Lithorous. Well this went little bit off plan, cause they end up attacking the one who was made to protect the island, the people.

"Smash" "Boom" and all sorts of attack started to initiate, but it dosn't seem to affect it a bit. He was taking down everybody like playing a child game, they were trying to stop his attack. Lithorous having the power of 7elements was burning, washing, blowing and making everyone unstable. He used one of his power which Ajax didn't knew about and there everyone in touch was down with black energy surrounding them. He was astound and confused, everybody was. People were dying and they were losing hope but something happened. He showed up, They hopes were dying but he came to restore it. The power of flames, with the magic it holds. He the legendary was here to save the night. Yeah you know "The Legendary Dragon!". He came flying, with his beautiful voice he kept them motivated, with the flames it cast, the enemy fears. He was here with the power of flames trying to slay the Protector. They all were trying their best when something happened! They could feel a vibration from deep beneath the surface of the island. What is happening their grandfather asked. Far away from them the Queen saw something, a demonic hand not looking like a humans, came out from the earth. She was worried, confused, vexed, pique and angry, she used every bit of power she holds to End the protector. She attacked him vigorously and it started to look she was overpowering Lithorous! Albert having the Axe and the strenght to use it was no exception. Athanasios was using all his power which was on other level and our man "Ajax" was a great deal in order to destroy him, not to mention the Dragon taking abnormal risk to protect everyone! But then again the intensity of the vibration from the ground could really be felt now. Here the protector was nowhere to stop and there a new problem was about to pop-up from the ground. Be ready everybody something is coming from beneath the earth Maya Suki shouted. From the beneath wait wait I think I got something! Beneath in the book It is written, "A Treasure one cannot imagine deep in the bore Adam's ale". That refers to the treasure hidden by you he said while pointing the Queen, and I have already converted in the mighty crystle Albert replied. Or so we thought! Ajax said. What if it never referred to it. Maya Suki said he has a point! Write beneath the well, there is a hidden place used to capture, the one powerful old man completed. Oh yes! We have a way to win this Athanasios announced. They made this fast in hurry and while still fighting. Ajax will go to the well, blast off the bottom and enlighten the room with his powers. While Maya Suki, Albert and Athanasois will make a curse. They have to make a curse covering all the things they need, A curse to powerful, to be the marked the Strongest and the first one to be made. This is a revolutionizing event one to be marked at the top of history! Making the curse while fighting the stout enemy needed a lot of Herculean and was not an easy task to do. But they have the back of all the creatures and humans. In these talks they got a little distracted and Lithorous turned his hand into a sharp pointy weapon. He was just a second away to attack them four when Ajax saved the day. He holding everybody used his powers to teleport them a little far from Lithorous. Yeah grandfather screamed and told "I knew you were the one who teleported us on that rainy night, I knew that!", She smiled and Albert was shocked of what he did. Ajax after reached the well and blasted the botttom of it with his lightening powers. But there there a mistake he made, a thing nobody thought off. When he brock the floor of the well and reached the secret, magical and unknown room made for the purpose of catching power. It snagged him inside and now he was stucked in the room, captured by the magic they had to use against Lithorous. It took them more than 10minutes to make the curse and now they hold equal power of it, means they have to attack him together. Ajax was suffering in the dark room as, A person dosn't dies because of the magic it holds but can never escape the place ever again until... They were done but still needed Ajaxs energy to magnify the power and effect of the curse. They were ready when the Dragon tried showing Albert what to do and he understood. The Dragon launched a strong and high amount of his Flame, distracting it. Then Albert told both of them to attack with full power right on his chest and so they did. The power of their attack was remarkable and it pushed Lithorous far in the sky, right in the claws of the Dragon. They all rushed to the place where Ajax was while their army fights the one made by Lithorous illusion but something was more. The Dragon dropped him down straight in the well and they three jumped after he was dropped. Lithorous breaked a part of the falling wall, in the downwards straight path and saved himself from falling in. They three falled right in his face and backed off instantly, hanging from the stones comming out of the circular walls. They all were seeing Ajax suffering and covered in pure dark energy. Oh no we needed your energy brother what did you do Albert yelled. Lithorous started attacking and they thought the game is over now but. Ajax saved the day (yes it was 5:34AM so almost day). He focused in the center of his head and gave all the power needed infact more, to the curse the Queen held in her hands. The energy was too much and it was still bright(energy), It was really a big deal for Ajax to do these all. Now as the curse was ready it distributed itself to everybody and them with their hands conjured the curse in the center of his chest. It was very powerful and caused him to fall down when their grandfather screamed "Now". He was going to go for him himself but then he saw the Queen do it. She rushed towards Ajax, seeing this Athanasois knew what to do, he made a energy ball very very strong under a second. She was there, she hold his hands and pulled him up, that was the exact moment he launched his energy ball. The energy and force from the explosion made the dark energy inactive for a second. Which was enough time for them to escape, and now together they see Lithorous getting trapped forever but that is not it. They have to escape and fast, something really bad could happen. Dragon called them up and when they were he threw a big rock in the well blocking it with the danger inside. The rock didn't touched the bottom, cause the well wasn't wide enough for it. It is all over Athanasois celebrated as the skies got brighter, some minuted until proper day! The Queen let them know that it isn't over yet. They all rushed to the place they were fighting and saw 20 demonic creatures, they were Demon themselves, good thing his army was gone. Oh no! The stone and Text bought together to open the wall that binds! she said. Albert you have to go and seperate the Text stones(that they found behind the Ancient Text) and the big one fast, and it will take a lot of power so use your brain she said. Albert rushed and did what was told too, it wasn't difficult when to seperate from behind. Albert teleported with the help of his grandfather and was back again and now another fight starts in this "War". A one sided fight! Dragon and team were way too strong for the Demons. Yeah they all ran for them and exactly one minute it took, to the third fight to get over. Mainly because of the Sun many demons become weaker in-front-of Sun. The Queen let them know that their shield didn't worked but we won together. So is it all over now Athanasois asked. We have it back, Our Pride! Thank You! she replied. Yeah we did it Ajax screamed and they celebrated. Ajax and Albert asked the Queen what next, while Athanasois meets his friends? Well I have a Kingdom to build! she replied!

ΔΔΔ

It was time, we see Ajax reading a book in terror, nah no horror book. He hears a sound of people screaming and when he comes up the thing he saw was different. The Ghosts of Graveyard flying dead all around the place!

About The Author

Sukhvir soni! A 13 year old Author and a multi talented person. I am a great learner and interested in space and technology. I admire to learn Philosophy, Astronomy and Alchemy with everything I can about science. I am active of many social media platforms and know how to code a little bit. I follow the Trend of crypto and NFTs as it is a really good thing to own. I like to spend my time read various types of books.

Printed by Libri Plureos GmbH in Hamburg,
Germany